NEW

By:
K K Mallender

www.kkmallender.com

Illustrated by: M C Johnsen

Published by:
 Rochester Media

Acknowledgements

This book is dedicated to John and Phil

I d like to thank the following people who were
very supportive during this project:

John and Phil
Gram, Cathy and her family
Mary and her family
My friend Jean
Chris and Jeff for recommending Rochester Media

Special thanks go to MC Johnsen for her illustrations.
I am looking forward to us working together again soon.

And I would like to thank Rochester Media for
making this possible.

Published by:
Rochester Media LLC
P.O. Box 80002
Rochester, MI 48308
248-429-READ
www.rochestermedia.com

Author: K K Mallender
Publisher: Rochester Media
Editor: Jessica Snyder
Illustrations: MC Johnsen
Cover Design: K Woodard Graphics

First U.S. Edition Year 1st Edition was Published

Summary: Ann Taylor, a fourth grade girl, experiences a new town, a new school, and new friends as her family moves to another state.

ISBN: 978-1460936672

1. Fiction, Family Life

For current information about releases by K K Mallender or other releases from Rochester Media, visit our website: http://www.rochestermedia.com

Table of Contents

CHAPTER ONE

The Move

Even surrounded by her closest friends, Ann Taylor felt totally alone. It was Tuesday, her very last day at her old school. The class had put together a party, sort of a send-off. As kids volleyed balloons back and forth, stuffed cupcakes topped with thick blue and white frosting into their small mouths, and wished her the best of luck at her new school, Ann grew sad.

She would miss these kids she had shared everything with the last three and a half years.

She would have to learn a new address and phone number, she would have to learn all new TV channels and she would have to make all new friends. No one could do this for her, not her parents, not her sister, Marie.

On the way home from her last day at her old school, Ann lost a tooth. Her tongue had been wiggling that thing for a week. As Ann walked in the door, she presented it to her mother.

"About time." Mrs. Taylor said. "I was worried it was going to fall out on the road and be lost."

One of her final memories would be in her old room finding money under her pillow when she woke up.

Wednesday was moving day. The van showed up early that morning and boxed up everything the Taylor family owned.

Ann and Marie each packed a small suitcase with a couple of changes of clothes, pajamas, their combs and toothbrushes and a book or two that they could use until all the moving boxes could be unpacked and the things put in their proper places.

Ann was in charge of King, the family's dog. She hummed softly and stroked his soft tan fur as the pug slept in her lap. Marie slept beside them as Ann's parents drove the family Buick from Indiana all the way to Missouri. Ann watched farm houses, open fields, small churches and tiny towns pass by her window. Nothing looked familiar, and she knew that nothing would be the same again.

At last the Taylor car pulled into a driveway and parked.

"We're here," Mr. Taylor announced.

"What do you think?" Mrs. Taylor asked. She was obviously excited. Her girls had not yet seen the new house.

Marie sat up, rubbed her eyes. "Cool," she said as she reached for the door handle.

Ann just stared, nervously fingering King's braided leather leash. Slowly she got out of the car and followed her family to the front door, King at her heels.

The one story red brick house with lots of windows looked nice enough. It looked a lot like the other houses on this street.

Together, Ann and Marie walked through the front door.

"Which room is mine?" Marie asked as she hurried off down the hall towards the bedrooms. "I claim this one," Marie called.

Ann followed her sister's voice and found Marie sitting on the floor of the closet in her room of choice.

"Great closet, don't you think? Your room's across the hall." Marie pointed over Ann's shoulder.

The two rooms were identical except Marie's windows faced the back yard and Ann's faced the front yard.

Ann went and sat in the closet in her new room, but she sat there only a moment. Seemed like the closet in her old room. *Why is that closet so special?* Ann thought to herself as she headed for the kitchen.

"The moving truck's here," Mrs. Taylor announced.

The furniture had been put in the truck last so it could be unloaded first. Mr. and Mrs. Taylor ran from one room to another showing the moving men where to put their things.

"Stay out of the way, girls," Mr. Taylor instructed.

Ann, Marie and King moved from room to room trying hard not to be in the way, but it wasn't easy.

After the table was in place, the girls and the dog headed for the kitchen. Ann tied King's leash to a chair leg and then the girls climbed up onto the counter with their legs criss cross applesauce.

"We won't be in the way up here," Marie said.

Mrs. Taylor brought King's water dish and a bag of paper cups from the car.

"Please give him some water," she said.

Marie reached across the kitchen sink, turned on the faucet and filled the bowl. Ann hopped off the counter, took the dish carefully from her sister and set it down next to her pet. King lapped the water up noisily, snorting and grunting, his curly-Q tail flopping back and forth.

As Ann climbed back onto the counter, Marie got an idea.

"Hey, Ann, let's see if Missouri water tastes different from Indiana water."

"Should it?" Ann asked her big sister.

"Don't know, let's do a taste test."

Again Marie turned on the faucet. She grabbed two paper cups and filled each one half way, then handed one to Ann.

The two girls stared at the water for several moments.

The water looked the same. Marie drank first.

"Definitely tastes different," Marie declared.

Ann was not sure she wanted it to taste 'different'.

"Go ahead, try it," Marie said.

Ann took a sip. This water did taste different. Ann had always thought that water was water.

While all the furniture and boxes were being carried into the right rooms, King slept under the kitchen table and Ann and Marie drank several cups trying to get used to the taste of the new water.

After everything was unloaded and the moving van pulled away, Mrs. Taylor unpacked just the boxes that had 'bedding' written on top. The Taylor family made their beds, climbed into them and tried to sleep. It had been a very long day.

Ann lay alone in her new room, where even her own furniture didn't look familiar. Her new school uniform hung on the back of the chair. At least she would be dressed like everyone else.

King was in his bed in the kitchen, Marie was across the hall, and her parents were at the end of the hall, but Ann still felt like something was missing; she just wasn't sure what.

Ann closed her eyes and tried to sleep. Tomorrow was a big day, the first day at the new school.

CHAPTER TWO

Mrs. "Kanyou…"

Mrs. Taylor walked the girls the two blocks from their new house to their new school. She took them into the office to fill out some paperwork and then left them with a tall thin woman wearing the name tag: Mrs. Meyers, Assistant Principal.

"They'll be fine, Mrs. Taylor. School lets out at 3:00. You can pick them up then."

"We can walk, Mom," Marie said. "I paid attention. It is such a short way."

"Are you sure?" Mrs. Taylor asked.

"Noooo!" a voice inside Ann's head screamed. But Marie nodded.

"Ok, I'll see you girls at home then." And their mother left.

Mrs. Meyers pointed out the cafeteria, the bathrooms and the media center. "If you need to know where anything else is, just ask..

"Every child who is not in his or her classroom when the bell rings," Mrs. Meyers explained, "must have a note from the office or they will be marked tardy.

"If a student doesn't come to school at all, they will be marked absent," she continued. "These marks will go on their permanent records."

Ann's eyes were big as saucers as Mrs. Meyers listed other rules that if broken would leave lasting marks upon their records. She wanted to keep her record clean. Had she had a record at the old school? Had she ever been absent or late? Had she ever failed a class or talked back to a teacher? Ann couldn't remember. She wasn't even sure what a permanent record was.

Ann pictured a huge poster with her name on it on the wall of the office. One column labeled 'good', the another labeled 'bad'. She pictured Mrs. Meyers with a big black permanent marker making marks in Ann's 'bad' column.

Marie was barely listening, she was not worried. She was a sixth grader and knew that their mother always got them up in plenty of time to have breakfast, to get dressed, to collect their book bags and get to school way before the first bell.

She also knew that the Taylor girls were only allowed to stay home from school when they were sick. Marie had never broken rules at her old school; she knew that her permanent record was clean.

Mrs. Meyers motioned the girls to follow her down the hall.

"Give that to your teacher," Mrs. Meyers said as she handed each of them a small square of pink paper. EXCUSED TARDY was typed at the top and Mrs. Meyers' signature was scribbled on the bottom.

"First door down on your right," the assistant principal pointed down the hall, "It says, Mrs. Jones, 6th Grade right on it. Go on, Marie, she is expecting you." And Marie took off towards her new classroom and never looked back.

"Four doors down on your left," Mrs. Meyers pointed out for Ann, "is Mrs. Kanuczynsqui's 4th Grade room."

Ann did not move. How many doors? Mrs. Kanyou... -what? "Go on, she's expecting you," Mrs. Meyers added.

Ann's tongue kept finding its way to the empty spot where her tooth used to be. Nervously she tried to feel for the replacement tooth, but there was no sign of any.

Slowly, Ann's feet began to move. Her shoes felt like

they were made of iron. Lifting each one up and down took great effort as Ann slowly walked down the hall. These halls looked just like the halls of her old school, same tan tile and brown brick, same worn black speckled linoleum floor.

All Ann could think about was why Marie had such a short walk and got Mrs. Jones and she walked almost the whole length of the hall and got Mrs. "Kanyou-something." Ann hoped she would know the name when she saw it.

The first door on her left had a sign that read "3rd Grade. Mr. Wright . The second door on her right didn't have any sign on it. She forgot to look at the second door on her left and by the time she reached the third door on her left, she had lost count, but that door said 2nd Grade. Ann kept walking. Why did the hall have to be so long?

The fourth door did say "4th Grade" on it, but there wasn't a teacher's name on the door. What had Mrs. Meyers said that the teacher's name was?

Ann stood staring at the door for several moments.

"Go on in," came Mrs. Meyer's voice from down the hall. "They're all waiting for you."

Ann drew in a deep breath, reached for the knob on the classroom door, turned it slowly and walked in.

A hush fell over the rows of students. The door opened up into the back corner of the room. The back wall was covered with brightly colored coats hanging on hooks. One side wall was made up of windows, but Ann couldn't make out what was outside. The other two walls were decorated with paper covered bulletin boards and green chalk boards.

Ann turned and faced the front of the classroom. She walked by all the other 4th graders sitting at attention in their wooden desks. She walked right up to the teacher's desk, presented her note of excused tardy and waited.

CHAPTER THREE

Attendance

"Class," Mrs. Kan-you-pay-attention announced. "This is our new girl, Ann. Everyone welcome her."

All together the class chanted, "Hello, Ann."

"Go hang your coat on any of the empty hooks." Mrs. Kan-you-find-a-hook pointed to the back of the room.

Again Ann had to walk by the all faceless students to get to the coat hooks. She slipped off her parka and hung it on a hook right in the middle.

"You will sit in front of Gail." Mrs. Kan-you-find-a-seat said as she motioned towards the student desks.

Which girl is Gail? Ann thought, but was too shy to ask. Ann began to move slowly. Great, she thought. My first minutes in this new class and already there's a test. Can the new girl find her seat? She felt twenty-eight pairs of eyes watching her every move.

The room was filled with white shirts, navy pants and navy and green watch plaid skirts. Except that half of the children were boys and half the children were girls, Ann's new classmates all looked the same to her.

Ann saw three empty desks. One was at the end of the fifth row. This desk was not in front of anyone so it could not be her new place. One was in the first row, in front of a dark-haired boy who looked even taller than Marie. The last empty desk was in the middle of the third row in front of a girl with a head full of dark curls and a spray of freckles across her nose.

"Hi, my name is Gail," the curly haired girl whispered as Ann took her seat.

"Hi," Ann replied shyly. "I'm Ann."

"I know," Gail giggled. Ann's face turned tomato red as she sat in her desk.

Ann tried to lift the lid on her desk to see what was inside. But the top wouldn't open like the desks in her last school.

Another giggle came from behind her. "Everything's down there." Gail pointed to the small storage area under

Ann's seat. Ann leaned over and saw several text books, notebooks and a pencil case full of pencils, erasers and a small ruler.

"Jim Abbott?" The teacher read out from the list of names on her desk.

"Here," a small voice answered from across the room, Ann wasn't sure exactly who said it.

"Patricia Burr?"

"Here," chirped the girl two rows over.

Ann knew this. Mrs. Kan-you-say-here was taking attendance. She would read out each student's name in alphabetical order. Those who answered "here" were and those who did not answer were marked absent.

Ann smiled at this familiar practice. This she knew how to do. She turned her head this way and that to try to match the names with the faces as the teacher sped through the alphabet.

"Gail Hamilton?"

"Here."

That, Ann knew was the girl behind her.

"Alan Johnston?"

"Here."

"Penny Phillips?"

"Here."

They were moving too fast. Most of the time Ann couldn't see who was answering so she gave up trying.

"Ellen Swanson."

"Here."

The names were starting to run together now. What letter was she on now? Was she getting close to T? Was she even going to read off Ann's name anyway? It was obvious to everyone that she was there.

"Ann Tyler?"

Ann's ears perked up. There was another Ann in this class. Ann was a common name, but she had never had one in her class before.

Quickly, Ann flipped her head back and forth eager to see what this girl looked like. Perhaps they would become friends, play at each other's houses, and swap books and Barbie clothes. Her sister Marie had a friend in their old school named Mary. Marie and Mary were as close as sisters, doing everything together. Could this Ann be a friend like that?

"Ann Tyler?" Mrs. Kan-you-hear-me said louder.

Still no response, the other Ann must be out sick. Their meeting would have to wait for another day.

"Ann Tyler?" The teacher's voice grew stern. Then in a loud command she bellowed, "New girl, stand up."

Ann stood straight up. The little hairs on the back of

her neck did too. Several of the kids chuckled.

"I am taking attendance, Ann. Do you know what that means?"

"Yes, ma'am," Ann said politely. She tried to stand tall even though her knees were shaking.

"When I call your name, you say "here"."

"Yes, ma'am."

"Were you paying attention?"

"Yes, ma'am."

"Then why didn't you say 'here'?"

"You didn't call my name," Ann said very softly.

"Speak up child."

"You didn't call my name." Ann said a little bit louder, but she could not keep her eyes off her shoes.

"Let's try this again, Ann Tyler?" The teacher stared at her new student waiting her reply.

"That's not my name." Ann said trying to keep her voice from cracking, while her eyes began to fill with tears.

"What?" The teacher yelled as the windows shook and plaster dust sprinkled down from the ceiling. Ann had never before met a woman with such a booming voice.

Mrs. Kan-you-understand-me looked down at her sheet and then back at Ann. Ann just wanted to sit down. She could feel all the eyes of her new classmates burning holes into her. She tried to wish herself back to her old school, back to her old classroom where the teacher spoke softly and knew her name.

"You are not," Mrs. Kan-you-be-kidding lifted her reading glasses that hung on a chain around her neck up to her eyes and read again. "Ann Tyler?"

"No, ma'am," Ann said trying to fight back tears.

"Then what is your name?"

"Ann Taylor," Ann squeaked.

"Taylor? Hmm, pretty close, Taylor, Tyler," the large woman rubbed her chin looking again at the list on her desk. "My mistake, let's try again, Ann Taylor?"

"Here." Ann answered, the room cheered and Ann's face turned red, again.

"Sit down Ann Taylor, not Tyler. It's time to get to work."

CHAPTER FOUR

Bumble Bee

Ann survived the first part of the morning by keeping her head hidden in her books. She found a nice surprise when she opened the geography book. It was the same one they had used at her old school. Unlike her last teacher, Mrs. Kan-you-turn-to-page-one-twenty-two skipped around so Ann wasn't exactly sure what they had already covered and what chapters were still to come. Ann hoped she could keep up.

Math is going to be easy, Ann thought as she looked over a worksheet covered in problems that she'd already mastered months before.

At 10:15, a bell rang and all of Ann's classmates jumped out of their seats, raced each other to the back of the room, grabbed their coats, flooded out into the hall and then out onto the playground.

"Gail and Ann," Mrs. Kan-you-hear-me bellowed and she waved the two girls up to her desk. "Come here for a moment, please."

Gail bounced her way to the front of the room with Ann following slowly behind.

"After recess, we're going to have a music test," the teacher began. "Even though you haven't been here, Ann, I'd still like you to take the test."

Ann put on her worried face, but neither Gail nor the teacher noticed.

"Gail has a solid "A" in music."

Gail grinned, showing all her teeth.

"Gail, honey, why don't you let Ann study your notes during recess."

Notes? Music notes? Ann was very confused.

Gail skipped off to her desk and brought back a loose-leaf page with writing on both sides and handed it to Ann.

"Gail, go out and play." The teacher pointed out the window. Gail grabbed her coat and was gone before Ann knew what was happening.

"Go, sit, read over her notes."

Ann returned to her seat and began to read. Lucky for her, Gail had very nice penmanship.

MUSIC NOTES

Beethoven - 5th Symphony - Sounds like thunder - I can feel the thunder - lots of thunder and then like wild horses running through a forest to avoid lightning striking trees. They are going crazy trying to get free

Mozart - Marriage of Figaro - Sounds like dancing children

Grieg - Peer Gynt, The Hall of the Mountain King. -From that old movie about the fairy tale guy who sings that inch worm song and then falls in love with the dancing mermaid who doesn't love him back

What? This didn't sound like any movie she had ever seen. Ann looked up at her teacher. The woman's face was buried in a book. Mrs. Kan-you-take-a-joke had to be kidding. Was she really expected to read over these notes during recess and then pass a test? There were so many and without hearing any of the music there was little chance Ann could pass this test. There wasn't enough time even if all she wanted to do was memorize what tunes went with what artist. Ann kept reading.

Tchaikovsky - Waltz of the Flowers - Sounds like the wind blowing through the willow trees.

Ann began to tremble. She read the sheet over twice before the wave of kids flooded back into the classroom. Ann handed back Gail's notes.

"Any help?" Gail asked.

"Oh, sure," Ann lied.

After the class had settled in their places, Mrs. Kan-you-get-a-pencil stood up and Ann gasped As she watched the tallest woman she had ever seen hand each student a sheet of paper. The sheet had three columns on it.

"Put your name on the test."

The first column was a list of numbers 1 to 10 with two blank lines next to each number. The second column was a list of letters from capital A to J by the names of songs that had been listed on Gail's sheet. The third column was a list of small letters from a to g next to composer's names. There were more songs than people so some of the people must have had more than one song.

"Listen to the piece," came the instructions. "Choose the title and the composer and put them in the appropriate blank. When you are finished answering each piece, set your pencil down so I can move to the next selection."

Ann fought back tears, but the tears were winning.

"As usual, no looking on your neighbor's paper." Then Mrs. Kan-you-perform-miracles looked right at Ann when she said, "If you don't know the title or the composer, guess. A wrong answer is better than no answer. At least you have a chance to get it right."

Mrs. Kan-you-stand-the-stress took out a leather case and flipped through it until she found what she was looking for. She put the CD into the player on her desk and hit the select button three times.

The music started slowly with simple piano. It was soft and romantic and although Ann had heard this music before, she had absolutely no idea the name or the artist. She kept listening while the other students were writing but no one else looked confused.

All at once the clatter of pencils on desks filled the classroom. Ann set her pencil down without writing anything.

Mrs. Kan't-you-even-guess played each musical selection with the same result. All the students, except Ann, scribbled their answers and set down their pencils. When number eight was playing, as she had with number 1 thru number 7, Ann read over the list of songs, but this time, one caught her attention.

The music Ann was hearing really did sound like bees flying and buzzing about. *"The Flight of the Bumble Bee"*, that had to be the right choice, but she couldn't figure out who wrote it. She remembered seeing it on Gail's list, but there had been so many names on that list, they sort of all ran together. She just guessed.

After the last piece was played, all the students except Ann set down their pencils. That is when Ann went to work filling in all the blank spots. She made sure that she had not used a title more than once and that each composer had been used at least once and then she set down her pencil.

At least that was over. Ann was sure that she had failed the test, but at least no one else knew it. Then something horrible happened, something that had never happened at her old school.

"Class," Mrs. Kan-you-listen's deep booming voice startled Ann. "Get out your red pencils and pass your test to the person to your left and we will correct them. People in the far row, walk your test over to the first row. The sound of crinkling papers filled Ann's ears as her paper was passed over to a boy whose name she didn't even know.

"Number one," The teacher began. "Number one is "Moonlight Sonata", D by Beethoven g."

As the other answers were read, the students circled wrong answers with their red pencils.

"We went over this material very thoroughly over the last few weeks so I trust you all did very well." The teacher said. "18 or more correct is an A. 16 -17 correct is a B. 14 -

15 a C, 12 – 13 a D and 11 or less correct is an F. Those of you with an F, if there are any, must take the test home and have your parents sign it."

A couple of students moaned. "No exceptions," the teacher replied. "Make sure you bring it back tomorrow, or you won't get any credit for taking the test. An F is better than a zero, my young friends."

Ann's face grew hot. The paper she corrected from Mike Evers had two red marks on it. So Ann drew a big red A on the top center of his test.

"Pass the papers back to their owners."

Ann's paper appeared on her desk while she was passing back the one she had graded. She couldn't look at the boy who corrected her test because she couldn't take her eyes off the big red F on the top of her own test. Ann had gotten only two answers right. Number eight was the "Flight of the Bumble Bee" and the first piece was composed by Beethoven, a lucky guess.

Not only had Ann been forced to take a test when she hadn't been taught any of the material, she was now expected to take the test home and get it signed. An F on her first test, what a great start at the new school. Could things get any worse?

CHAPTER FIVE

Lunch

Lunch was uneventful. Ann picked a seat over by the window and no one sat by her. She knew that after she finished eating that she could go outside on the playground with all the other kids. Maybe she could find Marie and at least have someone to talk to.

Her mother had put a special treat in the bag with the American cheese on wheat sandwich and bag of Ruffles. There was a full sized Hershey Bar – no nuts, of course. This school was a 'nut free environment'. Ann pulled it out and set it on the table beside her sandwich. It was a nice surprise, but Ann didn't feel like eating her sandwich. She didn't even feel like eating her treat.

Many of the other kids were in line buying milk. Ann's mother had given her money for milk, but Ann didn't want to stand in line with all those strange kids. They were chatting and laughing as if they had stood together in that line all year.

"One day you will look back on these first days and laugh," Ann's mother had told her over breakfast. "All the strange faces you see today will be great friends before you know it."

Ann looked around the lunch room at the kids talking and giggling. Except for their haircuts, Ann couldn't tell them apart. She recognized Gail and the boy to her left from class, but that was it. At this moment it was hard for her to believe that any of these kids would ever have her over to their house or even sit with her at lunch. Ann's eyes stung as tears invaded them.

After several minutes of staring at her food, Ann pushed her chocolate bar and her Ruffles into the center of the table. *Someone else can have them*, she thought. Then she put her sandwich back into the paper lunch bag and left the table.

Ann walked over to the trash can and tossed in her bag, uneaten sandwich and all.

The playground was mass of activity. The swings were full, the slides had a parade of kids going up and coming down. There was a group of boys kicking around a soccer ball in one corner and a group of girls doing the same in another. There were three games of hopscotch, two of jump rope, and several clusters of kids standing around talking. There was also a handful of kids who were chasing each other. Was this a game of tag?

Ann felt more alone on this playground surrounded by dozens of kids, than she did sitting all alone in her own room .

Ann strolled over to the jump ropes. She stood close, but not too close. Ann wanted to hear the rhymes the girls were chanting but not look like she wanted to join in. No one jumping rope noticed her.

"Miss Mary Mack...Mack...Mack, all dressed in black...black...black, with silver buttons...buttons... buttons, all down her back...back...back." Even though she had never jumped rope to it before, Ann knew this Miss Mary Mack rhyme. She had learned a one-on-one hand clapping version. Maybe she could join them. But would they let her? Suddenly Ann felt a light tap on her shoulder. She spun around to find Marie and another girl with long, dark hair grinning at her.

"Ann, this is Kim. Kim, this is my sister, Ann." Marie was out of breath from playing.

Kim nodded and smiled. Ann forced a smile back.

"How's it going?" Marie asked.

Ann's heart ached. Why couldn't she be more like Marie? Why couldn't she drop into a new school and make instant friends?

Before Ann could answer her sister, she felt another light tap on her shoulder. Again she spun around to find a thin girl about Ann's height wearing a navy parka and a bright green scarf. Her hair was pulled into two tight braids and she was smiling hard.

"Hi Kim," the girl said. Kim nodded.

"I'm Marie Taylor."

"I'm Bridget, Bridget Malloy."

"And this," Marie pointed to her little sister.

"I know. This is Ann Taylor, not Tyler. We are in the same class. I sit one row over, two seats back."

"Hi," Ann said softly trying to picture where this girl sat. She couldn't recall seeing her before.

"Hi, back at ya." Bridget said still grinning. "Did you just move in yesterday?"

"Yep, just yesterday," Marie said, but Ann just nodded her head.

"I think you live by me. Hey, Ann, do you want to walk home together after school?"

"Sure she does."

Ann was stunned not only by the invitation, but by her sister's response.

"Good, I'll meet you at the coat hooks. Don't forget." Bridget tapped Ann's shoulder lightly again and ran back to her soccer game.

"Why did you tell her we'd walk home with her?" Ann asked her big sister.

" You're going to walk home with Bridget. I got invited over to Mary Ellen's house."

"Who is Mary Ellen?"

"A girl in my class."

"Shouldn't you ask Mom first?"

"Mary Ellen's house is right across from the school. I'll walk over there and give Mom a call."

Ann said nothing.

"It's not like I'm spending the night. I'm just stopping by her house. It's right on the way home."

Ann admired her sister's bravery. She was scared to walk home with her sister for the first time, let alone with a girl she hardly knew.

"What happens if I get lost?"

"How can you get lost? We live less than two blocks from here."

Ann said nothing.

"Do you remember the new phone number?"

Ann nodded.

"Say it for me so I know for sure."

"555-0848."

"Excellent. Stick with Bridget. If you two can't find our house, call Mom from Bridget's house and Mom will come and get you."

"Marie?" Ann whined.

"What?"

Why can't the two of us just go home together? Ann thought, but didn't say. She did not want her sister to think she was a baby. Instead she said "See you at home."

Marie hugged her little sister and ran off to have some more fun before recess was over and Kim trailed behind. Ann walked slowly over to the door and waited for the bell to call them all back to class.

CHAPTER SIX

Walking Home

The rest of the afternoon was uneventful. The class took notes, read out loud, did some in-class work and copied down the lessons listed on the board that were to be done at home.

"Don't forget to have any failed tests signed by a parent and returned tomorrow," Mrs. Kan-you-believe-what-I'm-making-you-do said.

After the final bell rang, Ann gathered up the books she needed to take home and headed to the hooks at the back of the room. She stood watching the other kids grab their coats. She wanted to be sure when she went to reach for her coat that she was not grabbing someone else's by mistake. So many of the coats hanging on those hooks looked a lot like hers.

Ann also kept her eyes on three different girls with their hair pulled into braids. She wasn't sure which one was Bridget Malloy. In matching uniforms, it was hard to be sure. A quick prick of panic stuck her chest. What if Bridget forgot or changed her mind about walking home together? Without Marie, Ann wasn't sure she could make it home. She thought she should turn right after leaving the school parking lot, but maybe it was left? She just wasn't sure.

"Ready?" said Bridget.

"Sure," Ann blurted out as she grabbed her coat. She knew this one was hers; it had one of King's squeaky dog toys in the left side pocket. She'd put it in there for good luck. Ann picked up her book bag and followed Bridget out of the classroom, down the hall and out of the school.

Ann took several steps toward Bope Road before she realized that Bridget was headed in a different direction.

"This way," Bridget called out. "It's a short cut."

As they walked side by side Ann's stomach danced and her ears pounded as she tried to think of something to say.

What could she do to make this girl like her? Ann had no idea.

The sidewalk took a turn and disappeared into a hedge. Ann slowed, but Bridget motioned her to follow.

"This cuts between two yards and dumps us out onto Kenyon Road which we follow to Marlan Drive. They put this in to keep kids off the busy street."

Ann felt as if Bridget was speaking a foreign language. She was so lost. *I hope this girl knows where I live,* Ann thought to herself. She kept walking while fighting the urge to turn and run.

She could run back and try to find the way she'd walked with Marie this morning with their mother, but Ann was not even sure she could do that now. The school was no longer in sight.

The hedge on one side and the branches from overhanging trees along the other side made the walkway more like a tunnel. Ann thought it was creepy and exciting all at the same time. Once the girls made it through the tunnel, Bridget let out a triumphant, "See".

Ann had no idea what she was supposed to be seeing. In front of them were front yards dotted with trees and bushes just waiting to get their leaves. There were black-top driveways, each one marked by a single mailbox. Together the girls walked down a street lined with different colored brick homes, each one just a little different from the others.

"We turn here," Bridget pointed to the street sign which read *Marlan Drive.* "This is my street," the girl explained.

After passing five houses, Bridget turned and started up the drive of a house that, from the front, looked very much like the house that Ann had moved into yesterday with her family.

"This is my house," Bridget said. "That window there," she pointed to one of the front windows, "is my room."

"My room faces front, too," Ann explained and the two girls smiled at each other.

Bridget led her new classmate around the side of the house and into the middle of the backyard. She stuck her arm out straight and pointed at the yard that backed up to her own.

"There's your house," Bridget said.

Ann stared for a moment. There were bushes and trees and a built-in brick barbeque.

"That's your house, right? I saw the moving van yesterday."

Ann continued to stare. She had absolutely no idea if this was her new house.

"You don't know your own backyard?" Bridget asked with a giggle.

"We just moved in. I haven't been in the backyard yet," Ann explained.

Bridget and Ann stared a while longer.

"I could walk around and ring the front bell." Ann offered.

"Won't you feel stupid if some stranger opens the door?"

The girls stared at the house a while longer.

"Why don't we sneak up through the backyard and peek in the windows?" Bridget suggested. "You can check out the furniture and stuff and then see if you live there."

Ann thought for a moment. "OK," she said. This seemed like a good idea.

Slowly and quietly the two girls walked to where the backyards met.

"This way," Bridget motioned with her hand as she crossed into the other yard. Then she walked toward the back corner and Ann followed. They bent their knees and kept their heads down. They tried to stay as close to the ground as they could without crawling. The two girls snuck their way from tree to bush. They stopped for a few moments behind the brick barbeque.

"If this is my house," Ann said. "I hope my Mom doesn't see us. She'll think we are nuts."

Bridget laughed. "Oh, she'll just think we're playing some game. Then she'll open the back door and we'll know you live here. Come on, let's go."

The two girls pushed on. By the time they got up to the house, everything had grown. The door was so much bigger than it looked from Bridget's yard and the windows were so much higher off the ground. It was going to be much harder to sneak a peek than Ann and Bridget had imagined.

Together they stood under one of the back windows on tippy-toes and tried to look inside, but the blinds were drawn. They moved over to another window, but neither girl was tall enough to see the room inside.

Bridget backed away from the window and backed right into a large tree. Before Ann knew what was happening, Bridget was up on the fourth branch from the ground.

"Come on up," Bridget made a motion with her hand.

"I can't climb trees," Ann said sadly.

"I have three brothers," Bridget explained. "I had to learn a lot of things to keep from being left behind."

Ann smiled. Three brothers, she tried to imagine what that would be like, but couldn't.

"I see a couch, a TV and two chairs." Bridget described what she could see on the other side of the glass. "Looks like a coffee table and a whole bunch of boxes."

From what Bridget was describing, Ann couldn't tell if it was her family room.

"Anything else?" Ann asked.

Bridget climbed over to another branch to get a different view of the room. "Nothing," she said.

Ann took a deep breath and made her way up two steps to the back door. The top half of the door was glass and she crouched down under the glass and held her breath.

"Be careful," Bridget warned.

Ann slowly straightened her knees until she could peer into the kitchen.

"What do you see?" Bridget asked, "Anything

familiar?"

Ann looked around the kitchen. The refrigerator, stove and dishwasher didn't look familiar, but they all came with the new kitchen.

The table had so many boxes on and around it, Ann couldn't even tell what color it was. There was a rolled up rug leaning up against the pantry door, but it didn't look like the one in the old house.

Suddenly Bridget screamed and dropped from the tree and Ann turned and ran over to help the girl sprawled out on the ground.

"I'm OK," Bridget whispered. "But there is an ugly animal in that house. You must live somewhere else."

Ann stood straight up and looked into the kitchen just in time to see an excited King racing into the kitchen, his bug-eyes open wildly, his pink tongue curling out of the side of his mouth, and his curled up tail wagging back as and forth as he ran across the kitchen and out the door to the bedroom hallway.

Ann laughed. "That's my dog, King." Ann turned the back door knob, it wasn't locked.

"That's a dog?" Bridget asked. "It looks like a black and tan pig."

"Do you want to come in and meet him?" Ann asked.

"He's really sweet."

"Nah," Bridget said. "I'll come back when you get all unpacked. I'd better get home."

Ann opened the door and stepped inside. She turned to see Bridget running wildly past the brick barbeque.

"Thanks, Bridget," Ann called out. "Thanks for walking me home."

"See you at school tomorrow. Maybe we can walk home together again." With that Bridget disappeared through a line of bushes and into her own yard.

"Bye," Ann said softly to herself as she shut the back door and found her way to her new room.

CHAPTER SEVEN

Next Time

Ann started right in on her homework. She thought if she were busy at her desk, then her mother wouldn't be able to ask all about the first day at school. Ann couldn't even repeat her teacher's name. Except for the walk home, most of the day was a blur.

Ann could hear King running furiously through the house. *Crazy pug,* she thought to herself. She wondered if he did this when she was away at school. Then King flew into Ann's room and flopped down on the floor. He was breathing heavily from his sprint. Then without warning, King began to wheeze. He made deep gasping noises as if no matter how hard he tried, he couldn't get any air into his lungs.

Ann sat down beside him. As her mother had showed her the first time he had such an attack, Ann softly stroked the dog's back. She whispered into his tiny velvety ear, "Relax, you're just out of wind, breathe slowly."

"That's one of the disadvantages to having a pushed in nose," Mrs. Taylor had explained. "It makes it hard to breathe sometimes."

"You're OK, you're OK." Ann rubbed the dog's back until his breathing became normal and he fell asleep.

She got up and went back to her desk. A wave of panic went through her. She had to get the music test signed. Not only did she feel bad about failing the first test at this new school, Ann had to relive the whole thing again when she asked her mother to sign the page with a big red "F" on the top. She had never failed anything before.

Ann began to think of ways she could trick her mother into signing without actually showing her the bad mark. She could ask for her autograph. Ann could ask her mom to write her name on a piece of paper so she could compare mother and daughter writing styles. Ann didn't think her mother would fall for either of those.

She decided to wait until after dinner to talk to her mother. If she didn't get up the courage to ask, she would just sign it herself. It's not like Mrs. Kan-you-pull-this-off would recognize Mrs. Taylor's signature. Ann was pretty sure that the new teacher didn't get a copy of it from Mrs. Meyers in the office, or did she? Teachers could be tricky.

She would have to make sure for the rest of the year that she didn't need to get any other tests signed. Ann could handle that. But what about permission slips? What would she do if there was a field trip to a Science Museum or a Planetarium?

What if the faked signature looked a lot like her own? That is something Mrs. Kan-you-believe-it would notice.

Maybe, she thought, *I could ask Marie to sign it.* But the thought of explaining the whole music test disaster to her big sister, a sister who always got A's and who never got into trouble, was more than she could handle.

Just then, Ann's mother stuck her head in Ann's room. "How'd everything go today?" she asked.

"Great," Ann said forcing a smile. "Everything went great."

"Glad to hear it. I just knew it would." And her mother trotted down the hall towards a stack of unopened cardboard boxes.

Mr. Taylor called and said he would be home late so Mrs. Taylor served the girls dinner and then went to the master bedroom to do more unpacking.

Ann was very quiet at dinner as she sat across from Marie and picked at her food. The kitchen was very quiet except for the happy grunts as King nibbled his dog chow. Without any warning, Marie broke the silence.

"Failed your music test today, huh?"

"How did you know that?" Ann was shocked.

"I went over to Mary Ellen's house after school and her sister Patty is in your class."

"Great!" Ann said softly to herself. Not only was she a failure, but the whole class knew and was spreading this news to the outside world.

"Don't you have to get a parent to sign it?" Marie asked.

Ann nodded.

"Did you already show it to Mom?"

Ann shook her head.

"It won't just go away or sign itself."

"I know." Now Ann couldn't ask her sister to fake their mother's signature.

"Better to get it over with. If you wait too long you'll be in trouble for trying to hide it."

Ann knew she was right. So as soon as the girls rinsed their dishes and placed them into the dishwasher, Ann went to her room and got her test. The sight of the big red F on the top almost took her breath away.

Ann found her mother in the living room, standing knee high in crumpled packing paper. She was unwrapping the good china and stacking it in piles on the coffee table.

"Ann, honey," Her mother said. "Help me carry these into the kitchen. I should run them through the dishwasher before I put them away in the china cabinet."

"Sure," Ann said. She set the test on a stack of salad plates and headed slowly into the kitchen. Her mother followed closely behind with a stack of dinner plates.

"What have you got there?" Ann's mother asked as she watched Ann move the test from on top of the plates to a clear spot on the counter.

"I took a music test today."

"Didn't do very well, I see," her mother said as she picked up the sheet of paper.

Ann looked down at her shoes.

"Had to identify songs and composers?"

Ann nodded.

"Had you ever heard any of them before?"

"Some of them," Ann said softly.

"But you didn't know what they were called or who wrote them?" her mother asked.

Ann nodded her head.

"Get me a pen, please."

Ann ran to her desk, took a ballpoint pen from the top drawer and ran back to the kitchen. She handed the pen to her mother and then watched her scribble a few words on the top of the paper.

"Are you done with your homework?" Mrs. Taylor asked.

"Yes, all done."

"Can you do something for me?"

"Sure."

"Go into the family room, turn on the TV and see if you can figure out the channels. They are all different here. Write down what you figure out. I didn't have time to pick up a TV guide. Take your time and be sure."

Ann was all smiles. She had expected to be punished or at least scolded, but instead she was told to go watch television.

She reached up, hugged her Mom and gave her a quick kiss on the cheek. Mrs. Taylor smiled and then went back to her work.

Ann picked up her failed test paper and ran back to her room. As she set it on top of her book bag, she read what her mother had written.

She'll do better next time,
Mrs. Sharon Taylor

CHAPTER EIGHT

Trouble

The morning walk to school was uneventful. Marie and Ann walked the same way they had the day before, but this time Ann noticed all the houses they passed. Today she noticed the different styled mailboxes planted at the end of each driveway. She noticed old nests in the branches of trees. Had all these things been there the day before?

Through one front window, Ann watched a small white dog run back and forth across the back of a sofa, barking. She tried to remember if she'd heard a dog barking yesterday, but the whole walk to school was a blur.

Everything seemed different today. This was going to be a whole new day. Ann was almost excited. The teacher would know her name. All her homework was finished and ready to hand in. There would be no surprise tests. She might even have someone to sit with at lunch or jump rope with on the playground.

As they reached the school grounds, two older girls ran up to Marie. They were excited and giggling.

After a few moments, Marie glanced over her shoulder at Ann.

"Mary Ellen, Kathy," Marie said to her new friends. "This is my little sister Ann."

Ann smiled quickly and then looked down at her shoes.

"Hi, Ann," Mary Ellen and Kathy said together. "Nice to meet ya."

"Nice to meet you too," Ann squeaked out.

"Let's go." Mary Ellen said. And the three older girls headed off toward the stream of kids flowing into the school's front door.

"See you at home, after school," Marie said over her shoulder.

Ann wondered if she would be getting herself home or if she'd be walking home with Bridget. She walked slowly, glancing left and right looking for a familiar face or two. She hoped she would see one of the classmates she knew, maybe

Bridget or Gail. In their identical school clothes, Ann worried that she might not recognize them unless they were wearing their hair the exact same way as they did yesterday.

She saw no one, and no one came up to Ann until she entered the classroom. She slipped off her coat and reached out to hang it on an empty hook.

"I see you came back for more," a boy said. He wore the same navy blue pants and white button down shirt as all the other boys in the school. His blond hair was cut so short that at first glance, Ann thought he was bald.

"More?" Ann asked not knowing what he was talking about.

"Torture, school is torture. We do the same stuff every day, and we have to all do it the exact same way. Boring," the boy pointed both thumbs down. "School is sooo boring."

"Oh." Ann had no idea what this kid was talking about. She turned away from him and headed for her seat. Third row over from the door, third seat from the front, or was it fourth seat from the front. Good thing she'd left a yellow piece of paper sticking out just a bit so she could find it quickly.

"We aren't all the same, you know. Some of us need to do things our own way." The blond boy called after her.

Ann didn't turn around. She didn't remember this

boy's name, but she did remember him getting yelled at yesterday for talking while Mrs. Kan-you-be-quiet was talking.

The morning went by very quickly. Ann didn't ask any questions or volunteer any answers; she was just struggling to keep up.

Morning recess was the same as the day before. Ann stood close, but not too close to the rope-jumpers in hopes of being asked to join in. But she wasn't asked - maybe at lunchtime.

As Ann got in line to go back into the school, she noticed something in the far corner of the playground. A kid was flying a small kite.

She wasn't sure, but the kid could have been the same one who had talked to her by the coat hooks.

"Some of us need to do things our own way." Ann remembered his final words. Ann smiled and went inside.
Because it was Friday, Mrs. Kan-you-work-in-silence gave the class study time before lunch. The classroom was very quiet as the students worked quickly to finish any assignments, which if left undone, would have to be worked on at home over the weekend.

At one point Mrs. Kan-you-be-trusted left the room for a few minutes. Ann glanced around the room, but nothing changed. In her old school, one second after the teacher left the room, a rumble of excitement would have risen from the seats and at the very least, a paper airplane flying contest would break out.

Only one student moved. The blond boy from the coat hooks got out of his seat and walked over to the window. Ann watched him but was careful not to let anyone see her watching. The window he visited was only a couple of feet from his desk. He could almost reach out and touch it while he was sitting. Why did he get up?

With his back to the class, he turned the crank and opened the window. Ann couldn't see exactly what the boy was doing. His body blocked her view. After a minute, he cranked the window almost closed and returned to his seat. He had a piece of string in his hand.

Ann kept watching. Was that string left over from recess? At first she thought the string was attached to the window, but it reached over to the window and outside. Had this boy tied his kite to the window at the end of recess? Could it still be flying?

Ann squirmed in her seat. She stretched herself as tall as she could without getting all the way up. She needed to see if there was a kite flying at the end of that string.

The boy took the string in his hand and tied it to the

leg of his desk that was closest to the window. Every once in a while he would tug on the string and then shift it from side to side. All the while the string stayed tight.

Ann could not believe what she was seeing. Her classmate was flying a kite from his desk. *Some of us need to do things our own way,* Ann heard in her head again and it made her smile. She turned her attention back to her work.

After a few minutes Ann looked up and noticed that the teacher had returned. She had sneaked back in? Was this some sort of test? No wonder the kids were so good while she was gone. They never knew when to expect her back. *Pretty smart,* Ann thought. And even though she was still afraid of this large woman with a loud voice, Ann was beginning to understand her.

No one noticed when Mrs. Kan-you-believe-it rose from her seat and started walking towards the window. She moved slowly and quietly and stopped right beside the kite string.

"Mr. Minor," her voice boomed. The whole class looked up from their work. Mark Minor did not.

Mrs. Kan-you-all-see-this slipped a pair of blue handled scissors out of her pocket and held them high in the air for all too see. A soft gasp echoed through the classroom. Then in one swift motion she swung the scissors down and snipped through the string. In the center of the playground, a brightly colored object silently crashed to the ground.

Mark Minor didn't even flinch. He didn't move or even look up. It seemed to Ann like he'd expected to get caught. He was just trying to see how long he could get away with it.

"Come with me, please." Mrs. Kan-you-guess-what-happens-next said as she turned and walked back towards the front of the room. Mark Minor stood and followed.

"Front and center, Mr. Minor." Mark walked to the center of the open area in front of the chalk board where the whole class could see him clearly.

"Kneel, Mr. Minor." And Mark went down on two knees. A few kids in the back seats folded their legs up under their bottoms so they could have a clear view.

"Hands out, Mr. Minor."

Ann's heart began to pound. What was she going to do to him? Ann was shaking.

Mark stretched his arms out to his sides, parallel to the floor with palms up in a well rehearsed motion. *He must have done this before,* Ann thought.

The class watched as their teacher placed one textbook on each of the boy's hands, a math book on his right hand and a geography book on his left. Mark's arms dipped a little under the added weight.

"Class," the teacher said. "Go back to your work." As if any of these kids could focus their attention on their schoolwork instead of the boy kneeling in front of them balancing books.

"Do you have anything to say to the class?" the

teacher asked, but the boy said nothing.

Ann wondered what he was supposed to say. Was he supposed to say he was sorry for flying a kite out the window? Ann was pretty sure that she was the only kid who noticed until the scissors cut the string.

After a few minutes, Mrs. Kan-you-take-more put another book on Mark's left hand. "We must make this even." She mumbled to herself and she placed another book on his right hand. There was a low buzz among the children. From what Ann could hear, this was not the first time for Mark to be in this position, but it was the first time he got extra books.

Mark's arms bent at the elbows slightly at the new weight but his face didn't change. The class watched the clock. It was only two minutes until lunch. Could he last all two minutes?

After 30 seconds, tiny beads of sweat began to collect on Mark's upper lip. After one minute, tiny drops of sweat began to gather and slide down his forehead. After a minute and a half, his arms began to droop but he struggled to keep them high.

The bell went off and all the kids jumped from their seats, grabbed their lunches and their coats and flooded out the door. Ann followed them, but paused for a moment to see if Mrs. Kan-you-stand-it would hurry over to Mark and take the books off, but the teacher stayed behind her big desk.

Ann did not like this woman. She couldn't decide which was worse, holding up those books or having to kneel in front of the whole class. Thirty or so pairs of eyes watching, studying, judging, Ann could not have stayed up there as long as this boy had.

"Move along, Missy," the booming voice instructed, and Ann did just that.

CHAPTER NINE

Spelling Bee

Ann ate very little of her sack lunch. She sat alone again. At a table across the room she could see Gail, Bridget, Patty and two other girls talking and laughing. Ann had already been sitting when these girls chose their seats. She was not sure if they didn't want to sit with her or if they just didn't see her.

What would Marie do? Marie would get up, walk over to that table of girls and sit down with them, invited or not. She would say something cute or clever and a place would be made at the table.

The problem was that Ann couldn't think of anything cute or clever, and she didn't have the nerve to stand up and walk across the room. Ann played with her food by herself, in silence.

At recess she went over to the swings. Swinging was fun. It was something you could do all by yourself. But every swing had a kid sitting on it, flying back and forth, pumping their legs with all their might. Ann decided to check out the slide.

It was a tall slide, twice as tall as the one in the playground at Ann's old school. There was a huge line of kids waiting to climb the ladder and Ann didn't want to stand in a long line by herself. That would only make her feel more alone.

She spotted Bridget and Patty in the middle of the line, their heads leaning toward each other, talking and laughing.

Ann watched for a moment. She could wait until Bridget went down the slide and then walk up to her and then back with her to stand in line. Then she would be in the slide line with two girls from her class. Now this was a great plan.

Patty went down first. Whoosh, Patty flew down the slide. Her feet smacked the dirt pad at the bottom. She stood, then stepped aside and waited for her friend. Bridget flew down next. Her feet smacked the dirt pad, but she lost her balance and ended up falling to her knees.

Patty reached over and helped her friend stand and step out of the way before the next kid came barreling down. Bridget reached down and brushed the dirt off her knees. The two girls laughed and together ran off across the playground.

Ann's heart sank. Had they noticed her standing off to the side? Had they quit the slide because they hadn't wanted to include her in their fun? Or did they just decide to do something else, something that didn't require standing in line? Ann didn't know. She watched three more kids slide the slide and then she wandered over to watch the rope-jumpers.

When the bell rang, Ann went from the line to go into to her classroom, to her coat hook, to her desk without anyone saying a word to her. She noticed that Mark was not in his seat. Was he OK? Was he sitting in the office expecting to return to the classroom after a talk from the principal or was he sent home?

Once everyone was seated, Mrs. Kan-you-stand-the-wait made an announcement.

"It is Friday afternoon, class, and you know what that means."

There was a rumble through the room. Kids squirmed in their seat while they buzzed quietly to each other. They were obviously excited, but Ann had no idea why.

"Today's bee will be a triple elimination. Does everyone know what that means?" the teacher called out as she slowly paced back and forth in the back of the classroom.

"Three wrong and you're out," the class answered all together.

Ann's stomach tightened as she grew very nervous.

"Row one, take your places while I get the spelling list."

Spelling, in front of the class, out loud? What could be worse? Ann thought.

All the kids sitting in the row that ran closest to the door stood up, marched forward and made a line across the front of the room.

Ann's heart pounded. She did not want to have to stand up in front of all those strange kids and spell words out loud. There would be dozens of eyes looking her up and down waiting for her to make a fool of herself. She felt sick. She was a pretty decent speller but the spelling book at this school was very different from the one at her old school. Ann had always taken spelling tests on paper, never had she been in a "bee".

"Let's begin...left to right...ENGINEER."

"E-N-G-I-N-E-E-R" the first child spelled.

"Good, INJURED"

"I-N-J-U-R-E-D"

"Good, SEMICOLON"

"S-E-M-I-C-O-L-I-N"

"Wrong, strike one," the teacher made a note on her

clipboard. "Next, SEMICOLON."

The fourth child got it right.

For several minutes Mrs. Kan-you-spell-it-right shot words at the kids standing in front of her and each child replied with what they thought was the correct answer. If they were correct they stayed standing. If they got it wrong, they got a strike and after three strikes, they sat down. The last kid left standing was given a Tootsie Roll Pop and asked to be seated.

Ann's row was called up next. As she stood and took her place with the rest of her row, her stomach tried to climb out her mouth. She just wanted to sit down. With her luck, on her turn, Ann would open her mouth to spell her word and vomit would spray out on to the desk in front of her.

Ann waited for her word. Her tongue found its way to the spot of the missing tooth. She was sure there would be a gaping hole there for the rest of her life. She would be known as the new girl with the gaping hole in her gum.

Ann's heart was pounding so loudly in her ears that she could hardly hear the words.

"Dangerous"

"D-A-N-G-E-R-O-U-S"

"Hydrant"

"H-Y-D-R-A-N-T"

"New Girl," Mrs. Kan-you-spell-under-pressure said

and all the kids leaned in to see how this new addition to their class could perform. "Prefer". The teacher's deep voice filled the room.

Ann could feel dozens of eyes fixed on her face. Her mind went blank. "I just want to sit down," was all that ran through her mind. What was that word again?

"Prefer."

She could feel the heat travel up her neck and cover her face. She knew that she was beet red now which made her classmates stare even harder.

"P-E..."

"Wrong, next."

"P-R-E-F-E-R"

As the teacher moved from one student to the next, barking out words and waiting for a response, Ann could not help but notice the faces of the kids in their seats, the ones who had already been on the hot seat and were finished. They looked so calm, so happy to be out of the running, out of the spotlight, away from staring eyes.

"Awkward"

"A-U" Ann could see the a-w-k in her mind but the need to sit down was strong. She knew if she spelled three words wrong she could return to the safety of her seat.

"Wrong, spell awkward." Now Mrs. Kan't-you-spell-at-all was glaring at her. Her dark eyes burning holes in Ann's skin.

"A-W-K-W-A-R-D"

One more and this nightmare would be over. Ann tried to pay attention to the words being spelled around her, but the sounds of her pounding heart and her swallowing made it very hard to hear anything.

"New girl," Ann wondered if this teacher was ever going to learn her name. If she kept this up, the whole class, maybe even the whole school, would be calling her 'new girl' for the rest of the year.

Ann stood up as straight as she could.

"Failure" her third word was thrown at her.

This word was way too easy for her to fake spelling wrong. She would have to wait for a fourth word.

"F-A-L"

"Wrong, three strikes, you're out, sit down, spell failure" Mrs. Kan't-you-spell-anything looked disgusted.

"F-A-I-L-U-R-E"

Ann was shocked. She wasn't sure if she had done that on purpose or if it was an accident. As she took her seat, a warm wave of relief washed over her. She was the first person in her row to sit down, but she wasn't sad, she was thrilled. Ann looked around the room. All eyes were focused on the kids still standing. No one was looking at her, which was exactly what she wanted.

Ann's row was made up of pretty good spellers. It took quite a while to make all but one kid sit down. Still standing was Gail Hamilton. She took her prize Tootsie Roll Pop and sat down as the next row took their places in the front of the class.

Ann, her heart quiet and her stomach still, wrote many of the spelling words down as they were read to each speller. She wanted to make sure she knew them in case there was some sort of spelling test after the bee. With this teacher, Ann never knew what to expect.

After each row had its turn, the six winners, Tootsie Roll Pops in hand, took their places at the front of the classroom.

"Some of you did not do your best today." the teacher glared right at Ann.

Ann tried hard to swallow, but her mouth was too dry. "While some of you did very well, It took so many words to get to our finalists that we're out of time. We'll start with these super spellers next Friday."

There was a buzz of activity as each student got books and papers out of their desks to get ready to go home.

"When the bell rings, class, you are dismissed." The buzz got louder. "Have a nice weekend. Make sure you have copied the assignments due Monday from the board. If you did not finish work here, be sure to finish it at home, or else."

"Or else? Or else what?" Ann wondered.

Ann's head was down as she worked quickly to gather up her things. She had made it to the weekend and she was more than ready to go home.

Suddenly Ann heard a slap. She looked down at the floor and saw two huge, chunky black shoes parked next to her desk. Her eyes moved up the thick ankles to the wide black skirt, up the starched white shirt until she was looking at the underside of a rather bumpy chin dotted with fine gray hairs.

She jumped as she heard the slap again and realized that Mrs. Kan-you-be-deaf had her long square fingers spread across the top of Ann's desk. Ann stared in horror. Why was this woman slapping her desk?

"I see you are taking your spelling book home. Good thinking." The teacher slapped the desk again, and again, Ann jumped.

Peeking out from under one wide palm was a small white envelope. The teacher slapped the desk again causing Ann to let out a tiny gasp.

"Take this note home and have one of your parents read and sign it. Bring it back on Monday."

Ann just stared, her eyes as large as saucers.

"Do you understand, Missy?"

Ann nodded, her mouth still hanging open. She grabbed her things, grabbed the envelope, ran for her coat and then headed for the bathroom. She dumped all her stuff in one of the sinks, took the teacher's note and turned it over and over in her hands. The envelope wasn't sealed. The flap had only been tucked in so the paper inside wouldn't fall out.

Ann took a deep breath. She opened the envelope, took out the note and held the folded sheet out in front of her. She knew that Mrs. Kan't-you-mind-your-own-beeswax would never know and her mother wouldn't care so she unfolded the note.

It read: *Ann is a very weak speller. I am sending her spelling book home for the weekend. Please work with her over the next week. If she is still struggling next Friday, perhaps she can stay after school a few days so I can work with her one on one.*

Oh, no... not that. Ann's heart began to pound. What was worse? Spelling in front of a class of strangers or staying after school, one on one with Mrs. Kan't-you-remember-my-name. She wasn't sure. Right now they both seemed equally terrifying.

Ann started thinking about the empty desk by the window. Where was that Mark kid, anyway? Had he moved away, or was he at home recuperating from the book torture he had received at the hands of Mrs. Kan-you-believe-how-mean?

By the time Ann finished with the note, got her coat on, got her things together, and made her way outside she was the last kid on the school grounds.

Marie and Bridget were both gone.

"They're probably already home." Ann mumbled to herself as she started down the sidewalk, back the way she had walked that morning with her sister, but this time she was all alone .

CHAPTER TEN

News Travels Fast

Ann's poor spelling news made it to her house before she did.

"Were they words you hadn't seen before?" Ann's mother asked only seconds after she hung up her coat.

Ann wondered how her mother knew, but then she heard Marie opening and closing drawers in her room. Patty must have told her sister who must have told Marie. Great! By Monday the whole school would know. Instead of being called "The New Girl" she'll be called "Missy, the Poor Speller". That was just great! Maybe someone would write a story about it for the newspaper. The headline could read: *Girl Spells Badly, First Spelling Bee in New School.*

"When I was a girl, we used to make word searches and write stories using all the words in the week's spelling list." Mrs. Taylor rested her hand softly on her daughter's shoulder.

"Does that sound like fun, like it would help you with new words?"

"Sounds great, Mom." Ann's words said, but her tone said "I'm so sad and tired."

Ann fished the envelope out of her backpack and held it out for her mother.

"I need a signature for Monday."

Mrs. Taylor took the envelope, folded it in half and stuck it in her pants pocket without reading it. "You let me worry about that." She said as she patted her pocket. "Things will get better, sweetie," she said as she threw her arms around Ann, gave her a big squeeze, a quick kiss on the top of her head and then went back to her unpacking.

"Hope so..." Ann said softly but she was thinking *They can't get much worse*. She pictured herself spending the entire weekend copying over her spelling book.

"Ann," Marie called from her bedroom. "Ann?"

Ann knew what her sister wanted. Marie was about to offer her help. "I will quiz you day and night. Anything to help my little sister," Ann knew that was what Marie would say.

Ann hung her head and made her way back to her sister's room. She stood quietly in the doorway and watched Marie organize her drawers. Marie was amazing. She was putting the socks together by color. From the hall, the open drawer looked like a rainbow.

"Oh, there you are." Marie waved her hand. "Had some trouble in school today, I hear. If you need any help, just ask."

Ann started to turn towards her room. "I have been invited over to Mary Ellen Burns' house tomorrow," Marie said. "Her sister Patty is in your class. Anyway, I asked if I could bring you with me and her Mom said sure." Marie smiled and then turned back to her drawers.

Ann said nothing. This was not at all what she had expected her sister to say. Where was the talk about doing our best school work? Where was the talk about being prepared and staying organized?

"Well?" Marie asked.

"Well, what?"

"Do you want to go with me tomorrow? Mom said it was a good idea, that is, if you want to go." Marie waited. "Do you want to go?"

What else did she have to do on the first Saturday in this new place? No one else had invited her anywhere. Ann knew a few girls from school, but not well enough to be included in weekend fun. What else was there to do? She could sit around, read, watch TV, maybe copy over her spelling book. "OK," Ann said softly.

Ann went and laid down across her bed. This had been the longest week of her life. With her feet on her pillow, her chin resting on folded arms, she stared out her bedroom window. Everything looked so strange, so alien. Would she ever feel comfortable here?

Soon the clicking of little nails on the hall floor let Ann know that King was on his way. She didn't see him jump, but felt him land on her bed. He waddled over to her legs, turned three tight circles, dropped into a tight ball and fell fast asleep.

The tiny grunts and snores coming from the sleeping pug were the only things Ann found familiar in this new place. The tiny sounds that some people found weird or scary Ann found comforting.

CHAPTER ELEVEN

Come On Over

Ann walked with Marie one block past the school to the Burns' house. While she was standing on the front stoop waiting for someone to answer the doorbell, Ann began to get nervous. Maybe she wasn't welcome. Maybe she shouldn't have come.

"You sure it's OK that I came along?"

"You were invited."

Ann could hear the loud laughs and yells of many children.

"How many kids live here?" Ann asked.

"There are six Burns kids, but they always have friends over which can add up to a crowd."

A tall woman with curly red hair opened the door and smiled a wide smile at the sisters.

"Hello, Marie. This must be Ann."

"Hello," Ann said, half to herself.

"Go around back. Everyone is out in the back yard."

Everyone? Ann thought as she followed Marie around the side of the house towards the back. Ann took a deep breath as they rounded the last corner.

At first glance, it reminded Ann of Pleasure Island. That place in the movie Pinocchio where gangs of bad boys were promised carnival rides, ice cream, cigars and all the trouble they could handle.

There were six older boys playing roller hockey inside a tennis court and several older girls sitting on the ground watching them play. There were three little girls having a doll stroller parade. Two little girls and a little boy were working hard at digging a hole in a sandbox. Two boys were straddling their bikes trying to decide where to ride to next. Everyone seemed to be having fun.

This was just like Pleasure Island except all of these kids were wearing coats, hats and gloves; and Ann didn't think they would turn into donkeys before the day was over. Marie took off to join the hockey fans. Ann just froze. At first, she didn't see anyone she knew. A wave of panic washed over her. Maybe the kids she did know were right in front of her, but she just didn't recognize them. Maybe they were pretending not to know her.

Ann peeked over her shoulder. Maybe she could sneak away and go home. She could tell her mother that she had a stomach ache, that she didn't want Marie to miss out on all the fun, so she just came home on her own.

Ann peeked again. No one would notice if she just turned around and walked home, no one. Suddenly Patty, Bridget and Gail ran out of the back door, letting the screen slam behind them.

"Hey, Ann," all three girls said in turn.

"We're going to play jump rope," Patty said.

"Want to play?" Bridget asked.

Ann nodded and followed the girls over to an empty corner of the yard. Jump rope was something she knew. In fact, she was quite good at it. This was her chance to fit in, to be like the other girls. This was something the new girl had in common with these "grew-up-together" friends.

"Who wants to jump first?" Patty asked.

Gail and Bridget both screamed, "I do, I do."

"We'll hold," Patty said. "Ok, Ann?"

Ann nodded. She never minded holding the rope. That way she could listen to their jumping rhymes and see if she knew any of them. She knew a lot of rope-rhymes; maybe she could teach these girls some of hers. She was so happy until she looked at the rope.

It wasn't like the rope they used at school. In fact, it wasn't like any rope she'd ever seen before. Ann stood staring at the huge piece of elastic sewn together at one end to make a circle. She had no idea how to twirl a rope like that.

Patty stepped inside the circle and waited. Ann did nothing.

"Do you want to jump first?" Patty asked.

"No." Ann was so embarrassed. There was a long silence.

"Do you mind holding?" Patty asked.

"No," Ann answered, trying to fight back the tears.

"Well?" Patty, Gail and Bridget all stared.

"I don't know how to hold that kind of jump rope." Ann said softly pointing at the large elastic band resting limply on the ground. Once again she was different. Would she ever fit in?

"Oh," Patty laughed. "It's easy, nothing to it. Step inside the circle."

Ann did as she was told and waited.

"Now we hold the rope up to our ankles." Ann

followed the instructions. "Now you step back and I step back until the rope is tight, but not too tight."

Ann and Patty, the band around their ankles, stepped away from each other until they made a long thin oval.

"Stand with your feet apart, like this." Patty showed. "Now she'll jump."

"This is called a Chinese jump rope," Gail explained as she took her place beside the rope. "And you jump like this." She lifted her foot and placed it in the oval and then back out. She jumped in with both feet. She jumped over the oval and back.

"See," Gail said. "Easy." And then she started her routine.

Gail used a combination of steps to the rhythm of her jumping song. "One dark night, when we were all in bed..."

Ann and Patty kept their feet planted. Ann watched Gail's feet bounce up and down and in and out. Where did she learn how to do this?

Ann tried to watch Gail's footwork in slow motion, but she couldn't.

It was Bridget's turn. After Gail had a second jump, she took Patty's place holding the rope. After Bridget's second jump, she offered to replace Ann.

"I'd like to hold for a while longer." Ann said.

"Suit yourself." Bridget shrugged and took Gail's place holding.

After each of the girls, except Ann, had taken ten jumps, they decided to put the Chinese jump rope away.

"Are you sure you don't want to have a go?" Patty asked before she rolled up the elastic band.

"No thanks," Ann replied looking at her feet. "Next time." She would have to watch a little longer before she could risk making a fool out of herself in front of these girls. She wanted them to like her and no one likes a fool.

Without warning, all the kids in Patty's backyard began to rush over to the tennis court.

"Game!" Patty said excitedly.

Ann had no idea what was going on.

"You guys go grab us good seats, and I'll go get us something to drink." Patty headed off towards the house and Ann followed Gail and Bridget to the tennis court. The two girls sat on the cool ground outside of the tennis court just about half way from either end. Ann sat down near Bridget but leaving enough space for Patty to sit.

Ann watched the boys in the tennis court break into two groups. Roller hockey! They must be getting ready to play a game and all the other kids must be the fans. Ann grew very excited. She had never seen a roller hockey game before. She wondered which team to root for and decided she would just cheer whenever any of the kids cheered and not worry about choosing a side.

There was whooping and hollering as the boys skated back and forth across the tennis court. One side whipped the ball into the opposite goal and all the kids screamed. Then the other team scored, and the yard turned into a cheering crowd. When the game was over, most of the kids left for home. Marie found Ann and led her inside to thank Mrs. Burns for having them over.

"Come any time," Mrs. Burns told the girls as she walked them to the front door.

Once outside, Marie left Ann waiting on the front porch as she ran around back to say farewell to Mary Ellen.

Through the open door, Ann heard Patty's voice.

"I can't believe she never played Chinese jump rope before," Patty said. "Where is she from, Mars?" Ann's face burned red.

"You only learned last year," Mrs. Burns reminded her daughter and Ann said "Thank you" under her breath, so only she could hear.

CHAPTER TWELVE

An Invitation

Water pelted the windows so hard that it was impossible to see out. The cold never stopped the kids from playing outside, but the rain did. Having recess in the classroom was like not having recess at all.

Most of the class went to the gym to play volley ball. Ann didn't feel like playing, so she stayed at her desk to work on homework. The classroom was peaceful without a teacher and with only one student.

Ann was so engrossed in her reading that she didn't notice the other student who had come in and taken her seat. It was Gail.

After a few minutes, Ann heard soft little whimpers

coming from behind. She slowly peered over her shoulder and saw Gail, her nose buried in her math book, her eyes lightly leaking onto her freckled cheeks.

"Should I say something?" Ann wondered, "Or just pretend that I don't see?"

"Are you OK?" Ann finally squeaked out as she turned around to face her fellow student.

"No," Gail replied, wiping her eyes on the back of her hand.

"What's the matter?" Ann was afraid of the answer but asked anyway.

"I'm going to fail the math test on Tuesday." Gail blurted out.

Math, was one of the few subjects at this new school that Ann wasn't worried about.

"I had most of this stuff before. Maybe I could help you."

Before Gail could say anything else, the rest of the class poured into the room and hopped into their assigned seats.

"Class, class, class," Mrs. Kan't-you-be-quiet called out as she clapped her massive hands together.

Ann cringed at each thunderous clap.

"I have decided we should finish the final round of last week's spelling bee this afternoon so we can start with a clean slate Friday."

The buzz of excited students filled the room.

"Could the row winners from Friday please come up front and ready themselves for the final round."

Ann noticed that no one got up from the row nearest the window. Mike Minor must have been that row winner. His desk still sat empty. What had happened to him? Ann didn't ask anyone if they knew what happened to Mark. She wasn't sure she even wanted to know. Ann pictured him in the dark, damp, spider infested basement of the school. She pictured him tied to a large dust covered pipe with kite string.

All the other row winners took their places in front of the class and Ann thanked her lucky stars that she was not one of them.

Each word spelled was harder than the one before as one by one students were sent to their seats. Then after 27 words, only one student remained standing. It was Gail.

The entire class applauded as Mrs. Kan't-you-all-be-this-good handed Gail a blue ribbon to pin on her sweater. In the center of the badge it read in shining gold letters BEST SPELLER OF THE WEEK with the name Gail Hamilton handwritten on the second line.

Gail beamed as she returned to her seat. Ann couldn't help but picture Gail's tearful face just an hour before.

No one is good at everything, Ann thought to herself as she watched Gail walk past her and take her seat.

Marie and Ann stood huddled together under a bright yellow umbrella as they watched their mother's car pull into the student pick-up circle.

"How was school today?" Mrs. Taylor asked as her daughters snapped their safety belts into place.

"Great," announced Marie.

"OK," admitted Ann.

"Ann, you've got plans this afternoon," her mother said.

"Plans?" Ann was puzzled.

"You have been asked over to the Hamilton's house for a couple of hours. You need help with spelling and..."

Spelling? Oh no, not again, Ann thought.

"And Gail needs help with her math. How does that sound?"

"Where does she live?" Ann asked.

"Not far from here. Gail's mother gave me directions. I will drop you off and then pick you up before dinner." Mrs. Taylor was calm on the outside but she was cheering on the inside. Ann had made a new friend.

Mrs. Taylor parked the car in front of a house not far from the school, but on a street that Ann and Marie had never been on before. There was a huge oak tree in the front yard with a wooden swing hanging from the thickest branch.

"Wait here," Mrs. Taylor told Marie as she waited for Ann to get out of the car. Marie gave an enthusiastic thumbs-up, before she pulled out a library book and began to read.

Ann was nervous as her mother walked her up to this strange door. Before they had a chance to ring the bell, the door popped open and a short woman with dark curly hair and twinkling eyes motioned them to come in.

"Welcome! I'm Gail's mother." She held out her hand to Ann first and then to Mrs. Taylor.

"I'll be back in an hour," Ann's mother assured her. "Have fun," and she headed back out the door.

"Thank you for doing this," Mrs. Hamilton whispered to Ann as she led her down the hall. "Gail is in her room studying. She'll be so happy you are here."

Gail was sitting at her desk. Her head was resting in her hands and her eyes were closed, but she wasn't asleep.

"Gail, Ann's here." With those words, the two girls were left alone.

"Hey, Gail."

"Hey, Ann," Gail replied without even trying to lift her head.

Now what? Ann wondered as she looked around the

room. She spotted an extra desk chair next to Gail's dresser, walked over and grabbed it. She set it down next to her classmate and took a deep breath.

"Feel like studying math with me?" Ann asked, remembering Gail's tears earlier that day. "We have a test coming up and it always helps me if I can study with someone."

Slowly Gail lifted her head. Her eyes looked weary, as if they had cried themselves out hours before.

"Sure," Gail said softly.

"Let's start by going over the homework," Ann suggested.

"What did you get for the one with the bus?" Gail asked as she flipped pages of the book lying open on her desk.

"The one with the bus?"

"This one – number 4," Gail said as she pointed to a story problem.

"Oh, number 4, I didn't realize it was about a bus."

Gail looked puzzled. "You didn't know it was about a bus? How did you do the problem?"

"At 3:07 pm," Ann read aloud, "city bus # 319 picks up 10 passengers from the corner of 1st and Elm. At 3:12 pm, at the corner of 10th and Elm, the bus picks up half as many passengers. At 3:17 pm, at the corner of 16th and Elm, one third of the passengers on the bus get off. At 3:29 pm, at the corner of 18th and Elm, 8 people get on the bus. How long does it take city bus #319 to go down Elm Street from 1st Street to 18th Street and how many people were on the bus as it made its way toward 19th Street?"

"Twenty two minutes, 18 people."

"How did you figure that?" Gail asked, trying to hold back her tears.

Ann thought for a minute. She thought about the math tricks that Marie had taught her a couple of years before. Ann wanted to organize her answer in her mind before she spoke. She figured she had one chance to explain this before Gail broke down into tears.

"First thing you have to do is forget about the bus," Ann explained.

Gail looked confused.

"Forget about the streets. All that is thrown in to confuse you. This problem is really very simple."

"Maybe for you."

"Can I write on this?" Ann pointed to a blank piece of paper in Gail's desk.

Gail nodded.

Ann grabbed her pencil and began to write.

"The first part of the question – the bus starts at 3:07 ends on 3:29, simple subtraction. Twenty nine minus seven equals twenty two...do you see that?"

Gail nodded.

"Now this is the important part. Every place you see "and" or get on, you add. Anytime you see less, or in this case, get off, you subtract. The fractions just ask you to divide, and times just means you need to multiply. Doesn't matter if it is about busses or people or streets – you just have to boil it down to an equation."

Ann continued to write.

"We start with 10. Then half as many get on. 10/ 2 =5. So we add 10+5=15. Then one third get off. 15/3= 5 so we subtract 15-5=10. Then eight get on. 10+8=18. Do you see?"

Gail nodded slowly. "That seems too simple. What about number 6, the candy store? "

Together Ann and Gail took each story problem and worked them down to a set of numbers and symbols.

"Let me do number 14 all on my own."

While Gail was busy working on her problem, Ann began to look around Gail's room. It was a very tidy room. The walls were painted a pale yellow. The bed, dresser and night stand were a matching light golden wood. There were no posters, nor photos on the walls.

Ann wandered over to a bookcase filled with books and knick-knacks. On the second from the top shelf was a small collection of blown glass creatures. There was a brown speckled duck, a golden brown lion, a white swan with an orange beak, a gray donkey, a black and white cat, a brown vulture and a yellow snake curled up and ready to strike.

"I collect those," Gail explained as she looked up from her math work.

"I really like them."

"I get them at Hubble's Gift shop. They have a couple dozen of them in a case by the front register. Can you come and check my work?" Gail asked.

Ann returned to her chair. The two girls hunched over Gail's work for a minute and then both came up smiling. Ann stood up and knocked over a stack of cards and envelopes from the corner of the desk that she had not noticed before.

"Sorry," Ann said as she and Gail scrambled to pick up the small squares from the floor.

"Sponge Bob Square Pants, this one is Sheldon J Plankton, he's my favorite." Gail held one of the cards up to show Ann. "My birthday is next weekend and these are the invitations. I have to write them up tonight. We're going ice skating."

"Ice skating?"

"Do you like to ice skate?" Gail asked her tutor.

"Never been, only roller skating," Ann admitted.

"You should, it's really fun, especially with a group of friends. Hey, do you want to go over some spelling?"

Ann thought about being honest. She thought about telling her new friend that she had spelled all those words wrong on purpose just so she could sit down.

"Sure," was all that came out of her mouth.

After 5 minutes of helpful spelling hints, there was a wrap on Gail's door.

"Your Mom is here, Ann. Time to go."

CHAPTER THIRTEEN

The Waiting

"She didn't come right out and ask me," Ann admitted, "but she showed me the invitations and asked me if I liked to ice skate."

"Well, we can certainly buy her a gift, just in case you get an invitation," Mrs. Taylor said.

"Oh, I'll get an invitation, I just know I will." Ann exclaimed. "And I know exactly what I want to get her."

Ann and her mother went to Hubble's Gifts and Ann went right over to the glass case by the register. Three of the shelves were dotted with small blown glass animals. There were the ones that Gail had in her room already, but there were so many more. Ann examined an orange fantailed gold fish, a black and white bald eagle, a yellow-green lizard, a red cardinal, and others.

The one small glass creature that caught her eye was a dark green frog with bright orange dots on his toes.

"This one," Ann told her mother as she pointed to the green treasure.

"Is this for you?" the shopkeeper asked as Mrs. Taylor paid for the frog.

"It's a gift," Ann announced.

"Then we'll wrap it up special." The shopkeeper said as she carefully wrapped the glass frog in tissue and placed

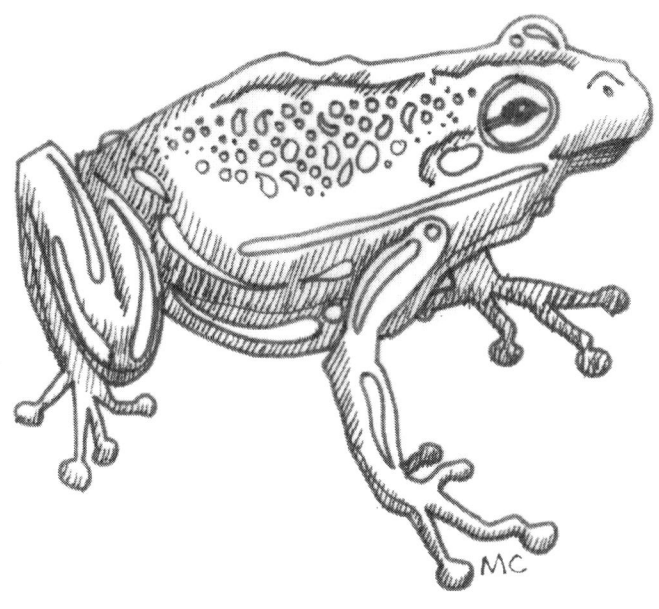

it in a small gift box. Then she tied a gold metallic ribbon around the box and tied it into a large bow that hung out over the top edge of the box.

"Perfect," Ann said to herself as she carried the present to the car; she was grinning so hard her face hurt.

On Tuesday, the school day crawled along. Every time Ann glanced up at the wall clock, only a few minutes had passed. All Ann could think about was getting home and checking the mail.

Ann decided to give up morning recess at least for a while. She knew she'd just spend it wandering around so she asked the teacher if she could stay in and study spelling for the next few days and, much to Ann's surprise, her teacher had agreed.

Before lunch, Mrs. Kan-you-do-any-better gave the math test. The classroom was silent and Ann figured that was a good sign. She did not hear one sob or moan from the desk behind hers. If she tried really hard, she could hear the gentle scratching of a lead pencil against test paper. Ann wanted Gail to do well on this test; she needed Gail to do well on this test. Maybe then Gail would think of her as her friend, her helpful friend.

At lunch, Gail, Bridget, Patty and several other girls carried their plastic orange trays covered in milk cartons, paper lunch sacks, napkins and chip bags over to the table where Ann slowly chewed her bologna sandwich. They talked about the math test and how Tuesday was the worst day of the entire week. Of course, they had said Mondays were bad the day before. Ann expected that tomorrow, Wednesdays would be the worst. No one mentioned the upcoming party. Ann just listened.

After recess, Mrs. Kan-you-figure-out-what-you-did-wrong walked up and down the aisles setting the graded math test in front of each student.

"Class," the teacher announced as she passed by Ann's desk. "For the most part, you all did quite well." Then she placed a test in front of Gail and added, "There was a noticeable improvement over the last test given."

As Ann slowly traced over her "A" with the tip of her index finger, her teacher's shadow covered her desk. Ann dared not look up.

After Mrs. Kan-you-put-your-test-away returned to her desk, there came a soft PSST from behind Ann. At first she thought she'd imagined it, and then PSST, she heard it again.

"I got a B" Gail's voice whispered into Ann's back. "That is the best I've done in math all year." Gail gently tapped Ann's right shoulder. "Thanks."

Ann's heart was pounding so loud, she could barely

pay attention to what was happening on the chalk board.
Ann had made a friend. Ann was going to go to a party, not because her sister or her mother got her invited, but because she made a friend.

After school, Ann raced all the way home. She hadn't waited to see what Marie was doing or if Bridget wanted to walk with her. Ann needed to check her mail.

Breathlessly, she pulled open the mailbox door and grabbed the bundle inside. There was only the usual collection of magazines and advertisements, no invitation.

"We surely get a lot of junk mail for only living here a few days," Ann said to her mother as she set the pile of mail on the counter.

"No invitation, huh," Mrs. Taylor said softly.

"Not yet," Ann chirped and headed for her room.

"It would take a few days to get here," her mother called after her.

On Wednesday, Ann had trouble concentrating. She kept imagining herself flinging open the mail box and finding a small square envelope with Ann Taylor neatly printed on it. Inside would be a picture of Sponge Bob, Patrick or even Sheldon J. Plankton and the words YOU ARE INVITED.

At lunch, several of Gail's gang announced that they had received their invitations so once again, Ann rushed home to check the mail. There were lots of envelopes, but nothing for her.

Even though there hadn't been an invitation in Wednesday's mail, Ann knew deep in her bones that there would be one on Thursday. Maybe Gail had to have her mother find Ann's address so her invitation was mailed later than all the rest. The Taylor family was not in the phonebook yet.

"The Taylors are not in the phonebook yet," Ann repeated to herself several times as she finished her homework. She said it aloud several times as she took a shower and several more as she got into her pajamas.

"Don't forget about our dentist appointments tomorrow," Mrs. Taylor reminded the girls as they stood side by side at their bathroom sink smearing toothpaste around their mouths with bent up plastic bristles.

"Wm hmmm remum mumm," the girls answered together.

"Best to get a dentist before there's trouble and you need one. No one wants to try to find a good dentist when they're in pain," she had explained to her girls.

As the sisters said goodnight, Ann almost told Marie about Gail's party. "Do you think I will get an invitation?" Ann wanted to ask her sister, but quickly changed her mind when Marie told her of her own plans.

"We have a field trip to the Zoo early Saturday morning, so a group of us are going to spend Friday night at Mary Ellen's, then all leave from there."

"A school trip, on Saturday?"

"Really early on Saturday the zoo gives tours of the things you can't see when the zoo is open; how they feed the animals and clean their habitat, how the hospital works, and how they take care of the babies. I think we even get to watch part of an operation. Mrs. Jones said that last year they got to watch a lion having a tooth removed. How cool is that?"

Without thinking, Ann's hands went to her mouth. She began to feel her jaw bones and her teeth through her dimpled cheeks.

"Cool," Ann said, but she was thinking about going to a new dentist. What if he found something the old dentist had missed? What if she had to have surgery and have teeth removed? And with Ann's luck, her surgery would become a field trip, so her whole class could watch the new dentist take out the new girl's teeth.

Before she got into bed, Ann went out to the kitchen and gently patted the beautifully wrapped gift waiting on the kitchen counter and set her hopes on getting her invitation on Thursday.

CHAPTER FOURTEEN

New Game

"This week, we are going to try something new," Mrs. Kan-you-believe-it announced to the class first thing Thursday morning. "We will not be having a spelling bee."

A low moan of disappointment filled the classroom, but a small 'hip-hip-hooray' filled Ann's heart.

"In preparation for the science exam next week," the teacher continued. "We will have a science quiz game."

A gentle murmur grew into excited chatter as the students waited for further instructions.

"Each row is a team and must pick a team leader. I will read a question. In turn, each team will talk over their response and the team leader will give their final answer. If a team gives the wrong answer, the next team is given a chance to answer correctly." Mrs. Kan-you-win turned and wrote the numbers one through five across the top of the board.

"I will keep score. Your team gets five points for a correct first response. The right answer is worth one point less each time an incorrect response is given."

A hand shot up from a boy in the last seat of the last row. Ann had no idea who he was. Had he been in this class the whole time? She had never seen him before.

"Question, Mr. Sullivan?"

"I don't get the one point less part."

"Row one gives a correct answer to their question, I award them five points. If they get it wrong, then row two gets a chance. If they get it right, they get four points, but if row two gets it wrong, then row three gets a chance but now a correct response is only worth three points."

Again there was a soft murmur throughout the room.

"Does everyone understand how we will be scoring this game?" Five rows of student heads nodded.

A hand shot up.

"Yes, Mr. Sullivan, you have a question?"

"Will the questions be multiple choice?"

"No, Mr. Sullivan," Mrs. Kan-you-believe-he-asked-that reached down into one of her desk drawers.

"This," she announced, "is my stop watch. Each team will be given 15 seconds to come up with an answer. Are we ready to start?"

"Yes, Ma'am," the kids chanted together.

Although she was still intimidated by the loud booming voice of her teacher, Ann felt comforted by answering in a team.

"I give you 30 seconds to choose a team leader."

Each row drew into a huddle and then jumped back into their seats. Gail had been picked in row three.

"Name an organ."

Row one huddled together. The last girl in the row stood and said in a firm voice, "STOMACH".

"Correct," and a five was scribbled under Row One on the board.

"Chloroplasts capture energy to make food from what?"

Row two huddled together. The boy who sat next to Ann stood and announced, "THE SOIL".

"Incorrect – next row."

Row three huddled together and Gail stood up and said, "THE SUN".

"Correct," and a four was scribbled under Row Three.

"What is the smallest unit of life in a living thing?"

Row four huddled together. A boy stood and announced "ATOM".

"Incorrect –next row."

Row five huddled together and the boy who had asked questions earlier said, without standing, "MOLECULE".

"Incorrect – next row."

Back to row one now. "CELL".

"Correct," and a three was scribbled under Row One on the board.

"Where is the hereditary material located in the cell?"

Row two answered "NUCLEUS".

"Correct," and they were awarded their points.

Row three readied themselves for the next question.

"Name two structures that plant cells have that animal cells do not."

In the huddle Gail suggested "CHLOROPLASTS and VACUOLES."

But Ann quickly corrected "CHLOROPLASTS and CELL WALL."

The other four members of row three looked at Gail.

"My bad," Gail said just before she responded with Ann's correct answer.

The game went on for over half an hour. The kids were clapping, cheering and learning.

When all the questions were asked and answered, Mrs. Kan-you-believe-the-winner called up the team leaders and had them add up their points on the board.

Row One and Row Three tied and all twelve kids were awarded a Tootsie Roll Pop.

Ann had a great time. The only thing that could have made this a better day would have been getting a certain something in the mail.

At lunch, Ann overheard Bridget and another girl that Ann didn't know talking about the skating party. Ann froze. She didn't want to be rude by listening in on the conversation, but at the same time, she really wanted to hear what they were saying.

Ann only caught only an occasional word.

"Gail...buzz...buzz...buzz...skating...buzz... buzz...buzz...pizza...buzz...buzz...last time..buzz...buzz."

Like a cold, wet hand, those last words hit Ann across the face. She knew at that moment that she was not going to get an invitation. Last time and the time before that and the time before that and the time before that, these same girls had celebrated their birthdays together, without the new girl, without Ann. Why should this time be any different? What reason would Gail have to include Ann this time?

Ann threw her lunch in the trash and returned to the

classroom. She never went outside for recess. If Mrs. Kan-you-go-outside had asked, Ann would have told her that her stomach was upset, not enough to go home but enough to stay inside. But the teacher never asked and Ann used the time to do homework and study science.

CHAPTER FIFTEEN

New Teeth

At the end of school, Mrs. Taylor picked Ann and Marie up from school and took them to an old house only a few minutes drive from school.

Ann thought the house was wonderful. It had an old fashioned wooden porch that ran halfway around. On the porch near the front door was a wooden swing hanging from the roof of the porch by two chains. It looked like something out of an old movie.

Next to the front door was a metal plaque that read: DR JOHNSON DDS

"Johnson, that's an easy one to remember," Ann mumbled to herself. "Why couldn't you teach 4th grade?"

Mrs. Taylor and the two girls went inside. While Ann and Marie were checking out the waiting room, Mrs. Taylor signed them in. The room was filled with big soft chairs that formed a circle around a wooden coffee table. There was a tall pile of books and magazines in the center of the table.

Ann spotted a toy chest off in the far corner and went to investigate. The toys were all too young for a 4th grader so Ann returned to the table and began looking for a magazine to read.

Marie was called first. When she was finished Mrs. Taylor was called. While Ann was waiting for her turn, all she could think about was how foolish she had been about the skating party.

"Why so blue?" Marie asked.

Ann shrugged her shoulders. She didn't want to tell her sister how foolish she had been..

"What would make you feel better?"

Ann thought a minute. "My birthday," she answered.

"That bad, huh? You'd need your birthday to cheer you up?"

"Or maybe Christmas," Ann added as her mother came back into the waiting room.

"Ann, your turn," Mrs. Taylor said as she pointed to the door.

"Is he nice?" Ann asked her mother.

"Very."

"I think so too," Marie added.

A tiny woman opened the door between the waiting room and the exam rooms. She was wearing cornflower blue scrubs covered with brightly colored fish and a name tag that read LOU. Why couldn't she teach 4th grade?

"Are you ready Ann?" she asked, a very small smile upon her very small lips.

Ann nodded and followed.

Ann was a bit disappointed, the rest of the office looked just like the old dentist office with big glass lights hanging over oversized lounge chairs and tiny spitting sinks next to each chair. She expected a new office to be totally different as her new home was totally different from her old one.

"Please sit here," instructed Lou as she pointed to one of the chairs.

Ann climbed into the chair and tried to make herself comfortable.

"Hello Ann," came a deep voice from behind the chair. "I'm Dr. Johnson." The dentist came around the side of the chair and stuck out his large hand for Ann to shake.

"Hello," Ann said as she shook the man's hand.

"Next time you come," the dentist explained, "Lou will clean your teeth, but with new patients I like to do the first cleaning myself."

Ann looked frightened. She had never had the actual dentist do more than look around her mouth, and make notes in a chart. Could this mean he was looking to take out a tooth like Ann had first imagined?

"Gives us more time to get to know each other."

"Oh," Ann said as she began to relax.

Slowly Ann's chair rose several feet into the air and then stopped with a sudden jerk. Dr. Johnson set a square bib on Ann's chest and fastened a cord on one side, around the back of her neck and then fastened it to the other side.

"What is your favorite subject in school?" Dr. Johnson asked as he slid a tray of tools over to Ann's chair.

"Math," popped out of Ann's mouth before she could even stop to think of what she wanted to answer.

"When I was your age math was my favorite too. You have to be good in math to be a dentist. Did you know that, Ann?"

Ann just shook her head. She tried to imagine herself hunched over a patient - her rubber gloved hands poking and prodding someone's teeth and gums. She could see drool sliding out the corners of the patient's mouth and onto the plastic backed bib.

"No," Ann answered, but she was thinking *I can't see myself doing what you do*.

She could see the dentist pretty well now as he sat on the stool next to her. He looked younger than her Dad. Dr. Johnson was tall and thin with dark brown eyes, the same color as his hair. Ann liked his hair.

But above all, Dr. Johnson had a kind smile and Ann knew, when he smiled, that he would not do anything to hurt her. That was a relief.

"First, we need to take X-rays." The dentist laid a heavy lead-filled apron on top of Ann's chest, set a piece of cardboard in her cheek and said, "Bite down and hold."

He pointed a large tube at Ann's cheek, stepped behind the chair and activated the machine. Dr. Johnson repeated this procedure until he had taken four pictures.

"I'll have those ready for you in just a few minutes, doctor.," Ann heard Lou say from the next room.

After the apron was taken away, the dentist worked on Ann's teeth. He gently poked and scraped; he tapped and polished; he squirted water and had her swish and spit. For the entire time Dr. Johnson cleaned Ann's teeth, he told her about his wife Laura and their new baby boy Sam.

"We have a dog - Lucy," the dentist explained. "We've had her for three years and have heard all sorts of horror stories about people bringing a new baby home, and the dog getting jealous and biting the baby."

"Wm knd rff rgg?" Ann tried to ask.

"Lucy is a basset hound."

"Wvv rhv arn ggug," Ann tried to say.

"A pug?"

Ann nodded.

"I love those dogs. They really have a lot of character."

Again, Ann nodded.

"Well, our vet told us to ignore the dog when the baby is sleeping and pay the dog extra attention when the baby is awake, that way Lucy will be thinking 'when will that baby be up so I can get attention'?"

"Rdd rtt wrkk?"

"We never got a chance to test it out."

Ann's eyes grew round.

"From the first moment Lucy smelled Sam, she became his shadow, his companion, his protector. She sleeps under his crib and if Sam cries in the middle of the night and one of us doesn't get to him quick enough, Lucy comes and tries to hurry us along."

Ann tried to smile even though the little mirror and pick were in her way. *What a nice man,* Ann thought, *for a dentist.*

One final rinse and spit and Dr. Johnson lowered Ann's chair. He unfastened the bib, wadded it into a ball and tossed it toward the nearest trash can. The ball went right in.

"Two points," Dr. Johnson's arms flew up in the air and Ann laughed.

"Now let's talk about your teeth."

Ann's throat tightened. She expected him to say "We need to dig one out. It is a very painful procedure but you seem tough – you can handle it." But Ann did not feel tough. Suddenly her tongue found its way to the hole that used to be a tooth. It had been days since she had remembered that there was a hole in her smile.

Just then Lou came in and handed her boss a sheet of what looked like black paper. Dr. Johnson rolled his chair over to the wall and hung the paper up. Then he flicked a switch and part of the wall lit up.

"Hmm," the dentist said as he rubbed his chin between his thumb and forefinger.

"Everything looks good, no cavities. Keep up the good work brushing."

Ann said nothing, her tongue still exploring.

"Do you have any questions for me?"

"Am I going to have a hole for ever?"

"The bicuspid?"

Ann looked puzzled, "bi-what-ed?"

"Bicuspid," he opened his mouth and tapped one of his teeth.

Ann nodded. "When I lost other teeth, there was always a tooth waiting to come in. I could feel it. This time there is just this big hole."

"Can you see that?" Dr. Johnson pointed to a light spot on the x-ray.

Ann nodded.

"That is your new tooth. It has a little ways to go, but before you know it, you'll have forgotten that old baby tooth had left a hole."

Ann looked doubtful.

"By the next time I see you even," Dr. Johnson said and he flashed Ann a kindly smiles. "You need some patience," the dentist said as he helped his patient out of the chair. "Don't be in such a hurry and things will come to you." *And that,* Ann thought, *could be said for more than just her teeth.*

CHAPTER SIXTEEN

Christmas In February

When the Taylor ladies came home, their teeth glowing and tingling from the dentist, Mr. Taylor was waiting.

"My beauties," he said as he scooped each one up in his arms and kissed them.. "How was the dentist?"

"Nice," the girls said together. "Mom stopped on the way home at Steak 'n Shake and bought us dinner.

"Was it good?" Mr. Taylor asked.

"Would have been better if our mouths didn't still taste like fluoride," Ann explained and her father laughed.

"Is it date night?" asked Marie.

In their old house, one evening a month, Mr. Taylor came home from work early and took his wife out on a dinner date. Gloria from across the street had come over for a couple of hours and played games while Mr. and Mrs. Taylor were out.

In this new place, now that the girls were older, Mr. and Mrs. Taylor were going to try to leave the girls by themselves.

"Phone numbers are on the pad," the girls were reminded.

"Ann, listen to your sister and do what she says. She is in charge."

"Marie, take good care of your little sister and you can call us for any reason. We won't be gone but a couple of hours."

"We'll be fine," Marie assured her parents as they locked the front door and walked down the walk and out of sight.

"What are we going to do?" Ann asked.

"Is your homework done?"

Ann nodded, thinking about her lunch time study hall.

"Good," Marie chirped. "You need cheering up so I was thinking we could either celebrate your birthday a bit early or we could have a Christmas Party."

"Huh?"

"Well, we don't have time to bake you a cake, find you a present, or send out invitations."

Ann took a deep breath as her eyes filled up with tears. Was the thought of a birthday invitation going to make her sad from now on?

"So," Marie continued. "I vote for the Christmas Party."

"How would we celebrate Christmas in February?" Ann asked.

"I'm not sure. How do you think we should do it?"

Ann thought for a minute and then it came to her like they had done this a dozen times before.

"We could put out a few decorations and put some Christmas music on the stereo." Ann began to get excited.

"We have half an hour to set up and half an hour to clean up, so that leaves us an hour to play Christmas. What do you say?"

"Let's do it," Ann cheered throwing her arms up in the air.

The girls went first to a storage closet in the basement and pulled out two boxes of Christmas decorations. They grabbed handfuls of garland, strands of twinkle lights and a collection of glittery bobs.

With Marie's help, Ann hung the smallest ornaments she could find on all of the house plants, strung garland and lights from curtain rod to curtain rod, hung stockings off the fireplace mantel and tied a Santa hat on to King's little round head.

Ann put on Christmas music and turned it up loud.

"What are we missing?" Marie asked her sister.

"Do you know how to turn the heat off?"

"Sure," Marie said as she ran over to the thermostat on the wall and hit a button. Two beeps and she turned to Ann. "Off, now what?"

"We open a couple of windows."

"It is freezing outside," Marie explained. "That will make it..."

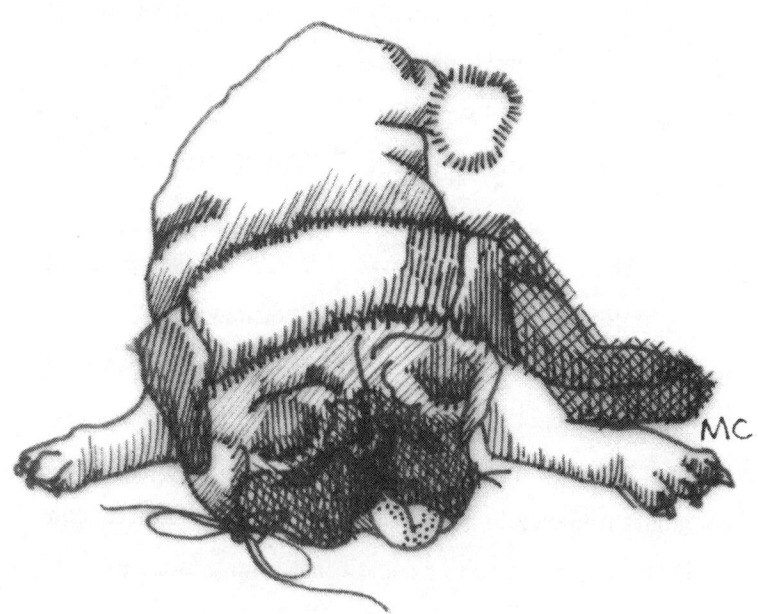

"Feel like winter in here," Ann finished her sister's thought. It didn't take long for the temperature in the house to drop so that the girls each put on a coat, hat, and scarf. Even King got a scarf.

"We need presents," Ann decided. She sat down, set her chin in her hand and thought for a minute. "Marie, you go and pick something from your room that you think I would like to have and I will do the same. We'll wrap them up and set them under one of the plants. Before we put all the decorations away we'll exchange gifts."

"Great idea," Marie said and the two girls went off to pick out a treasure. Each wrapped up their chosen gift and set it under the Norfolk pine tree that lived in a large ceramic pot in the corner of the living room.

For an entire hour the girls played Christmas. They went Christmas caroling; they pretended that each window in the house was the door of a neighbor and they sang two songs to each one. Even King played along. He didn't sing, but sat patiently next to them at each pretend house.

The girls sang and danced and laughed until they could barely breathe. Then it came time to open their gifts.

Slowly Ann opened the gift her sister had wrapped for her. It was a small wooden box that had belonged to their grandmother. Marie kept it in the center of her dresser.

"This is yours. Mom gave it to you from Grandma's things. I couldn't possibly take this. You love this."

"I want you to have it. She was your Grandmother too," Marie reminded her sister.

"Thank you – so very much. I'll love it forever."

Marie slowly opened her gift. It was a small framed picture of Marie and Ann when they were very young. Marie was sitting in a rocking chair and was trying desperately to hold Ann on her lap. But Marie was too small and Ann was too big, so together they fought sliding off the rocker. In the midst of the struggle both girls beamed with love for each other.

"Where did you get this?" Marie asked.

"I found it in a photo album and Mom made me a copy and helped me pick out the frame."

"I don't think I've ever seen it before," Marie confessed.

"I keep it in my top dresser drawer and bring it out if I get lonely; it perks me right up."

"What a great gift, just knowing this picture makes you happy is a great present for me. Won't you miss it?"

"If I need to look at it," Ann said pointing to her sister's room, "I'll know where it is."

After the girls hugged each other, they turned out all

the lights except for the ones strung with the garland. Then they sat together on the floor and listened to *Oh Holy Night* and *Silent Night* on the stereo.

Then Christmas was over. Together the sisters closed the windows and turned the furnace back on. They quickly collected all the decorations and put them back into the proper boxes.

In the center of Ann's dresser sat a small wooden box and in the center of Marie's dresser sat a small framed picture.

By the time Mr. and Mrs. Taylor returned home, the sisters were in their pajamas, sitting on the couch watching *The Wizard of Oz*.

"Move over," Mr. Taylor instructed his daughters. Marie, Ann and their parents sat together on the couch and, even though they had seen it a dozen times, the Taylor family watched the movie together.

"There's no place like home, there's no place like home," Ann repeated to herself as she fell asleep that night.

CHAPTER SEVENTEEN

Homer

On Friday Ann tried to stay to herself, but failed. In class, Gail kept poking Ann while they were working on Math homework.

"Psst," Gail hissed with a poke, poke, poke. "I totally get number three." And "Psst," Poke, poke. "Number four isn't as hard as I thought it would be."

Each time Ann nodded and without turning around, flashed a thumbs-up over her shoulder. Mrs. Kan't-you-do-your-own-work never seemed to notice.

At lunch, Ann went to one of the far tables over by the windows where no one else was sitting. Just as she pulled her peanut-butter and butter sandwich out of the bag, Bridget plopped down next to her and started talking.

"We haven't walked home together in a few days," Bridget said. "How about if we do it today?"

"Ok."

"Good," Bridget took a big bite out of her own sandwich. "I've got something I want to show you." The two girls ate the rest of their lunches in silence.

On the playground, Ann stood off to the side and watched a game of foursquare. After a while, she wandered over to the swings and watched.

The swingers were all girls, and all, Ann thought, younger than she was. They pumped their legs back and then stretched them forward, reaching as hard as they could towards the clouds. Back and forth they flew, their hair swishing, their skirts puffed up in the swinging breeze.

Ann stepped over to the slide and watched the long line of kids wait their turn, climb the ladder, and then whoosh their way to the ground. Next week, she vowed to join them.

Toward the end of the day, Mrs. Kan-you-work-quietly gave the class time to work on their homework. Ann worked very slowly. She was hoping to have a load of school work so she would be kept busy on Saturday.

While the kids were reading, writing and arithmeticing

their way through their assignments, Mrs. Kan-you-believe-I-am-still-talking walked slowly up and down the aisles. She talked about what they had learned over the week and what they would be working on come Monday.

Mrs. Kan-you-hear-me's voice was so loud that Ann wondered how anyone could concentrate. She wondered if she would ever get used to that deep boom of a voice.

Ann wasn't sure if it was her imagination or if the floor was actually vibrating each time that woman spoke. Ann kept her eyes down. She didn't want to attract any attention. Mrs. Kan-you-remember-my-name would crush her as if she were a tiny bug.

"What was this teacher's real name?" Ann said to herself as she continued to study the floor. She thought about the sign on the door, 4th Grade, but no teacher's name. One day she would need to know it, but hopefully that day was a long way off.

After school was dismissed, Bridget patiently waited for Ann to get her coat, hat and gloves on. The two girls walked out of the school and by the time they got through the shortcut, they had decided to skip the rest of the way. Laughing and out of breath, the girls arrived at Bridget's house.

"What did you want to show me?" Ann asked as she followed Bridget up her driveway.

"I guess it's more like a 'who'."

"Huh?"

Halfway up the driveway, a small girl with wild golden hair and a generous smile came running to greet them.

"Is he home?" the girl asked.

"I think so," Bridget said excitedly. "Ann, this is Kathy. She lives next door."

"Ah," Kathy said. "You must be Ann Taylor, not Tyler, the new girl."

Ann nodded and wondered why she had never seen this girl before.

"Kathy is a grade behind us." Bridget explained as if she had heard Ann's thoughts.

The three girls continued up the driveway and into the garage.

"This," Bridget announced as she pointed to what looked like a wet pile of brown and black rags, "is Homer."

Ann stared for a moment, her eyes still trying to adjust to the lack of light in the garage.

"Go ahead, you can pet him," Kathy said. "He's very sweet."

Ann kept staring. What were they talking about? And then she saw it. One end of the rag pile moved slightly and then she saw the other end blink.

This was not a pile of rags, but a dog; possibly the ugliest dog Ann had ever seen. His hair was thick and bristly and stuck out in every direction. His eyes were so dark that unless he was moving them, they were almost impossible to see.

As Ann drew closer, she could see that Homer was about twice the size of her King. She crouched down, stuck out her hand and let the dog sniff her. His tail began to thrash. Then very gently Ann stroked what she only assumed was the pup's head. His fur was rough but not at all wet.

"I don't really have any idea what you like," Bridget said. "But you have that really scary looking dog, so I figured you must like dogs."

As Ann slid her hand under his chin and gave him a little scratch, his tail thumped in a steady rhythm. Now

she could see the patches of wiry gray hair that decorated his muzzle.

"Hey, Ann, he likes you," Bridget announced.

"How old is he?" Ann asked as she moved her hand and began to scratch behind Homer's left ear.

"No one knows for sure."

"How long have you had him?"

"Oh, since I was in kindergarten, but we don't really own him."

"Nobody does," Kathy added as she slipped a small Milkbone out of her pocket and offered the treat to Homer. He tenderly licked her hand and then took the bone and ate it.

"What do you mean?" Ann asked.

"He sort of belongs to himself," Bridget explained.

"What?"

"Mom likes to say that he owns us. About five years ago, Homer just showed up at our door, like he already knew us. He didn't have any tags, in fact, he wasn't wearing a collar. We gave him some food and water and he just keeps coming back. Not every day, but whenever he feels like it." Bridget reached over and gave Homer a big love hug and he gave her face a quick tongue bath.

"We had him neutered. Now we take him to the vet once a year, you know, for a check up, shots and all that stuff.

We make sure his tags are current. We don't want some other family taking him to the vet."

"They could give extra shots," Kathy added.

"And that," Bridget said, "could make him very sick. We let him in the house, but he really likes to sleep here in the garage. If he's here when I go to sleep, then he's never here in the morning. Other families on our street put out food for him, but he always comes back to our home."

"Homer," Ann smiled.

"I knew he'd be here today. He's been gone since Monday."

"My brother is allergic to dogs, so I've sort of adopted him as my dog too," Kathy explained.

"Don't you worry about him? When he's not here, I mean?" Ann asked.

"Not really. My Dad says he's taken good care of himself for years. Why should he stop now?" Bridget grinned proudly.

Ann gave Homer a tender kiss on the space between his eyes. "He's very special," she told Bridget.

"Some of my friends don't like him. They say he's funny looking, but I thought you'd appreciate his other qualities," Bridget beamed.

That was one of the nicest things anyone had said to

her since the move and Ann was grateful. As she ran through Bridget's backyard and through her new backyard, Ann thought about something else Bridget had said.

"I really don't know what you like." And Ann figured it had been silly for her to expect an invitation. These girls had been close friends for years and really didn't know her at all. Just wanting to belong doesn't make it happen. If she hadn't seen those invitations, Ann never would have known about the party, never expected an invite, never felt left out. As Dr. Johnson had told her, "She needed to be patient."

As usual, Marie had plans after school, so when she walked through the back door, only her mother and King were there.

Mrs. Taylor was folding laundry and the pug was asleep under the kitchen table.

"How was your day?" Mrs. Taylor asked as she stopped her work and met her youngest at the back door.

Ann only shrugged. She set her backpack on the kitchen table. "Did I get any mail?" Ann asked quietly, already knowing the answer.

"I'm so sorry, honey." Mrs. Taylor wrapped Ann up in her arms and tenderly kissed the top of her head. Ann hugged back.

"Looks like it's you and me tonight," Mrs. Taylor

said. "Your Dad has to work late tonight and Marie is spending the night at Mary Ellen's. We won't see her until tomorrow night."

Ann said nothing. At least one of the new Taylor girls fit in.

"I thought we could do something special for dinner. What sounds good?"

Nothing, Ann thought, but said, "Whatever you want is fine."

"I thought tomorrow we could go to a movie. We haven't been to a theater yet in this new place. How does that sound? Or we could go to the mall, window shop, and maybe catch some lunch. What do you want to do?"

"Movie or the mall," Ann said softly as the wrapped present caught her eye. She walked over to the counter and gently tapped the box as she had done several times before. Her eyes filled with tears. Ann had never felt so lonely.

Gail was lucky, Ann thought. She's always in the center of things, in the classroom, on the playground, at other kids' houses. Bet she gets invited to a lot of parties. Just once, Gail should feel sad and dejected.

Suddenly Ann felt King's pushed-in nose investigate a small spot on her shin. His whiskers tickled and the corners of Ann's mouth turned up. His wet little nose moved from one spot to another as he investigated the smells Ann had picked up during her day. His tightly curled tail rocked back and forth with joy. The simplest things made him happy. Ann knew she would always have King.

Ann picked up the gift.

"I thought Gail would really like this."

"It is a very thoughtful gift."

"I know what I want to do tomorrow," Ann said as she placed the present back on the counter.

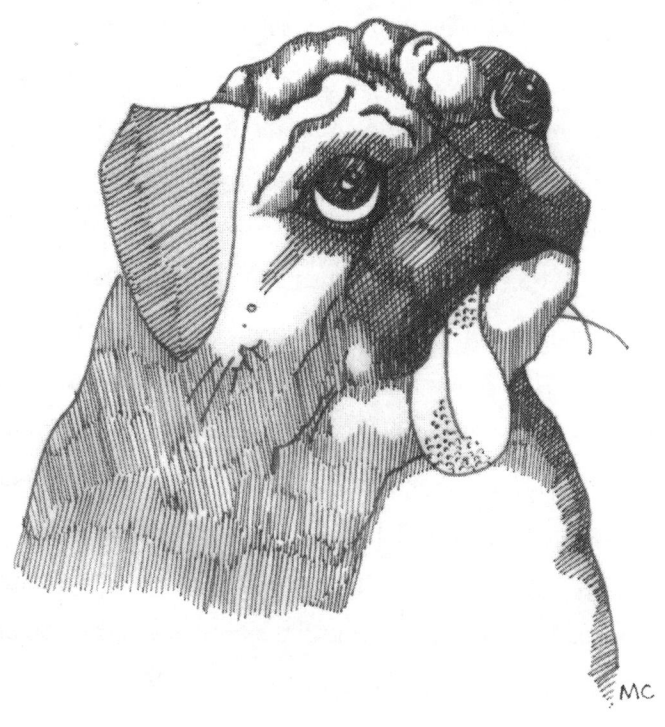

MC

CHAPTER EIGHTEEN

The Gift

"Do you want me to go with you?" Ann's mother asked as she stopped the car and put it in park.

Ann shook her head. "I need to do this myself." She took a deep breath, opened her door and stepped out onto the driveway.

This was the hardest thing she had ever done. Ann walked slowly up to the front door. She could turn and run, no one would have to know she had ever been there. Ann turned back to look at her mother. She knew if she turned and ran, her mother would not be angry. But Ann would definitely be mad at herself. This was her one chance to take a stand, make a statement, to get noticed.

Ann's hand reached out slowly and before she could change her mind, her finger pressed the bell. As the front door swung open, Ann could hear the cloud of laughter coming from the back of the house.

"Hello, Ann," Mrs. Hamilton said as she glanced over Ann's shoulder, saw Mrs. Taylor and gave her a quick smile and wave.

"I curd ti Ga," Ann cleared her throat. "I heard it was Gail's birthday today."

"How nice, dear. Do you want to come in?" Mrs. Hamilton opened the door farther and motioned for Ann to enter.

Ann shook her head. She reached into her coat pocket and pulled out the small wrapped box that had been waiting on the Taylor kitchen counter for days.

"I wanted her to have this." Ann held out one hand with the present balanced in the center of her palm. *Take it now, so I can run away,* Ann thought.

"Wait here," Mrs. Hamilton turned and went back inside without taking the gift so Ann had no choice but to wait.

In just a few seconds, Gail stepped out of the door. "Hey, Ann," Gail said.

"Hey, Gail," Ann took a deep breath. She didn't want to jumble up her words and end up feeling even more foolish than she already did. "I know it's your birthday, well, I wanted you to have this."

Gail said nothing. She just stared at the gift still sitting in Ann's outstretched hand.

"Do you want to come in?" Gail asked with a jolt of enthusiasm in her voice. "We're going skating. You could come with us," Gail grinned. She obviously meant this invitation.

"Thanks," Ann said as she handed the gift to Gail. "But my Mom and I are on the way to the movies."

"Oh," Gail's smile fell. She looked disappointed and a little embarrassed. She shifted her weight from one foot to the other as if she were uncomfortable. "Maybe another time," Gail said.

"Sure, another time."

"Thanks for this," Gail held the little box up in the air.

Ann smiled and then Gail smiled.

"Happy Birthday," Ann said as she turned and walked back to the car.

"Thank you," Gail said. "See you at school," she added.

"See ya," Ann gave a little wave over her shoulder. By the time Ann had gotten back into the car, Gail was back inside and the front door was closed.

Mrs. Taylor started the car and began to back down the driveway, but before the car was on the street, Ann began to cry. After getting out of sight of the Hamilton's house, Mrs. Taylor pulled over and parked.

"Not exactly what you expected?" Mrs. Taylor asked gently.

Ann shook her head.

"Did you think was she was going to invite you to her party?"

"No," Ann said softly. "But she did anyway."

"You didn't want to stay?"

Ann shook her head.

"Ann, honey, why are you so sad?"

"I bought that frog because I really thought I was going to get an invitation to her party," Ann confessed.

"And," her mother added, "Because you thought she would really like to have it."

"Yes, for her collection," Ann agreed. She was only sniffling now. "Then when I realized I wasn't invited, I thought it was because those girls didn't like me."

"And now?"

"I think she just didn't think of me. Those girls don't really know me at all."

"Why do you think that is?"

"Because I'm new here."

"And?" Mrs. Taylor encouraged, her voice still gentle.

"And we really haven't spent much time together."

"That's right. And does that mean you're not fun to have around?"

Ann shook her head.

"It just means that when they get to know you better, then you'll be invited to parties and over to play."

"But I feel like I know them. I would have invited all of them to my party."

"And why do you think you know them better than they know you?

Ann considered this.

"Besides my family, they are all I've got. But it takes time to make friends."

"It sure does."

"I need to be patient", Ann said as she thought about Dr. Johnson.

"That is a lot to learn in one day." Mrs. Taylor lightly rubbed her daughter's arm. "Do you feel better?"

Ann shook her head.

"What else is bothering you?"

"I really wanted to give her that frog, but maybe I should have given it to her at school, not here at her party."

"Why would you say that?" Mrs. Taylor asked.

"I'm afraid I made her feel bad that she didn't invite me."

"And you didn't want that?"

"At first, maybe I did." Ann looked down a little ashamed to admit this. "I thought that would make me feel better, you know, to make her feel bad. But not now, Gail didn't hurt me on purpose. She had no idea."

"And now you think she feels bad."

"Maybe," Ann admitted, her eyes welling up with tears.

Mrs. Taylor thought for a moment. "Well, just make sure that the next time you see her, be very nice. Act happy to see her, to see all the girls. If they talk about the party, ask questions but don't act sad, act interested."

"I'll try." Ann reached over and gave her mother a tight hug.

"Do you want to go to a movie? We have some time to kill before Marie and your father get home."

"Can we just go to the mall and walk around?" Ann asked.

"Only if you let me buy you lunch."

"Sure," Ann giggled as Mrs. Taylor put the car in drive and headed in the direction of the mall.

CHAPTER NINETEEN

Empty Desk

West County Mall seemed so familiar to Ann she could almost pretend, while she and her mother walked around, that they had never moved. The floor plan was a little different from the mall near their old house, but most of the stores were the same.

Ann and her mother decided on a small lunch in the food court instead of a bigger lunch in one of the restaurants. Ann got a grilled cheese sandwich and a chocolate milk shake from the A & W counter and her mother picked out a salad and iced-tea from Wendy's. It felt good to go somewhere and do something that didn't revolve around school.

Ann volunteered to bus their trays and while dumping

the trash and adding their trays to the stack of other used trays, Ann felt a tap on her left shoulder.

She spun around and found Mark Minor standing in front of her.

"Hey, Ann," he said grinning. "Remember me?"

"Hey, Mark." Ann looked him up and down. He looked healthy, unharmed. "How are your arms?"

Mark smiled, lifted his fists up as if to show off his muscles. "Good. You looked scared when I was kneeling there and I realized you didn't know that was the third time I've had to hold those books. It's a punishment I chose, the first time I caused trouble."

"You chose?"

Mark nodded. "The choices were, writing a paper, staying after school or a punishment of my own choosing. So I chose what I like to call 'the book balance."

Ann smiled. This kid really did like to do things his own way.

"When are you coming back to school?" Ann asked but then thought, maybe she shouldn't have.

"Back?" Mark grinned harder, "Never left. I just changed classrooms. After the kite incident, Mrs. Meyers decided that I should move across the hall into Mrs. Murphy's room."

"Mrs. Murphy's room?"

"She's the other 4th grade teacher."

Murphy, that's an easy name to remember, Ann thought.

"She's pretty nice, I guess. She thinks I get in trouble so much because I'm bored, so she's giving me extra work."

"I haven't seen you on the playground either," Ann stated, still picturing his empty desk.

"For the privilege of switching rooms I have to work in the office, before school, recess, and after school."

"How long?" Ann asked.

"Not sure. Until Mrs. Meyers gets sick of me hanging around, I guess."

"That stinks."

"Not really. I actually like working in there, but don't tell anyone. At that school, as soon as you start enjoying yourself, they find something else for you to do."

"They have me organizing the Lost and Found stuff, which is kind of funny because that's where I got that kite. Went looking for a lost glove and came out with a kite and a great idea." Mark laughed and Ann smiled.

"At the beginning of the year, Lost and Found starts out as a box. They get tons of stuff - hats, sweatshirts, socks, gloves, books, toys - all sorts of stuff, so much stuff that by this late in the year the box evolves into a closet."

"Ya know, there is an assortment of single boots in that closet. Makes you wonder what kind of a kid could lose one boot and not go to the office and try to find it. What can you do with one boot?"

Ann laughed, picturing a playground filled with one legged children playing hopscotch, jump rope, going down the slide.

"It's really quite interesting."

"Doesn't sound interesting," Ann admitted.

"Beats kneeling in front of a classroom trying to balance books on your palms," Mark said with a smirk.

"You can say that again," remarked Ann.

"Beats kneeling in front of a classroom trying to balance books on your palms," and the two 4th graders laughed.

"Got to go, see you 'round, Ann Taylor-not Tyler."

"See you 'round Mark-now-in-Mrs.-Murphy's-class."

"Who was that?" Mrs. Taylor asked Ann when she returned to the table.

Ann told her mother the whole story of Mark getting caught flying a kite out the classroom window and about the punishment.

"Sounds like that young man is better off in the other classroom."

Ann nodded. *Why couldn't I be in the other class*, she thought to herself?

"Ann," Mrs. Taylor waited until her daughter looked her in the eyes. "You aren't always going to like all of your teachers, or when you are out in the grown-up world, all of your bosses."

Was she reading my mind, Ann wondered to herself? "I know," Ann said.

"You're not only going to school to learn Math, English, History and other subjects, you are also there to learn how to work in a group setting and how to get along with all sorts of people, kids and grownups alike."

Ann thought about this.

"Those are lessons you will carry with you and use more often than that list of the Presidents you memorized last year."

Ann didn't want to admit to her mother that she could not repeat that list of Presidents one month after they'd been tested on it. It had seemed like such a big deal at the time.

Maybe, at recess one day next week, Ann would go to the office and try to find the missing boot she really didn't lose.If she ran into Mark, that would be great.

CHAPTER TWENTY

The Fall

"Psst," plus a tap on her shoulder made Ann turn around. "I have something for you, but don't open it until you get home," Gail said as she handed Ann a small square envelope.

"Did you guys have fun skating?" Ann asked with the widest friendliest smile she could manage.

"Sure did. Did you and your Mom enjoy your movie?"

"The one we were going to see was sold out," Ann lied. "So we shopped and had lunch instead."

"That sounds like fun. My Mom and I haven't done that sort of thing in a long time."

"Class," Mrs. Kan-you-feel-the-power-of-my-voice called out loudly.

Ann quickly turned around.

"All eyes and ears on me." Ann's hair blew back from the shear force of her teacher's voice. It made her shudder. The teacher came and stood next to Ann's desk as she explained the lesson they were about to begin. She rotated her body slowly so that everyone could hear her voice and see the serious look on her face.

Mrs. Kan-you-focus rhythmically tapped a ruler in her hand as if she were trying to decide which student she would smack with it.

Ann could barely pay attention. She felt like she and her desk were slowly shrinking under her teacher's gigantic shadow. Couldn't that woman stand somewhere else? Would Ann ever make it through this day? She began to watch the hands on the wall clock slowly find their way from number to number.

Ann spent the morning recess in the bathroom. She'd raised her hand to go just minutes before the recess bell and headed down the hall to hide. She did not want to spend recess time alone with Mrs. Kan-you-be-afraid.

Ann took a good look in the mirror.

"You will participate. You will not spend all your time watching. If someone asks you to play, you will play. How do you expect these kids to include you when you won't include yourself?" Ann lectured.

"Right, Ann? ," Ann said and she forced a wide smile.

Then she noticed something odd, something she had not noticed before. Without using her fingers, Ann lifted her top lip as high as it could go.

She was amazed. There in the spot that used to be a hole was the small white edge of a new tooth. Ann touched the edge with her tongue.

"Everything comes to him who waits," Ann's Grandmother used to say.

After lunch, Ann did her usual walk about the playground. She meandered from hopscotch, to jump rope, to foursquare without playing anything. As usual, Ann ended up at the slide and, as usual, the line was really long.

Ann got in line, but it was so long that she wondered if she would ever get a turn. From where she stood, Ann had a perfect view of the kids sliding down, bouncing up and then heading back to the line. The line moved slowly.

One by one, the kids whooshed down the slide, popped up and ran to take a place at the end of the line. *It is sort of an odd shaped circle,* Ann thought. After each child completed the circle, Ann took one step forward.

Ann was fascinated by the repetitive sounds of the slide. There were moans and squeals of glee; the hum of fabric rubbing against the smooth slide; the pitter patter of feet smacking the hard ground and then running around to the end of the line; all peppered with the light sound of children chattering amongst themselves.

Suddenly the rhythm was broken. Someone had stopped at the top of the slide. Ann was standing next to a support pole that was cemented into the ground to keep the slide from tipping over. She looked up to see who had stopped. She had to lean way over to keep the glare of the sun from blocking the slider's face.

It was Bridget. She was perched at the top. It looked to Ann as if she were waiting for someone.

"I'm taller than you, Patty Burns," Bridget giggled and leaned over the edge of the slide so she could see Patty waiting in line.

"Not for long, Bridget Malloy," Patty yelled back.

A cloud shifted and Ann looked down to keep the sun from poking her in the eyes.

Thud, splat and pop drew Ann's attention to the base of the pole. Bridget was lying on the ground next to Ann's feet. She had fallen from the top of the slide.

Bridget was lying on her stomach, her face white and she was gasping as if she couldn't catch her breath.

She's knocked her wind out, Ann thought. She bent

down, lightly placed her hand on Bridget's back and said softly, "Just relax, breathe slowly, you've just knocked your wind out." Ann gently rubbed Bridget's back until her breathing became easier. "You're OK, you're OK," Ann repeated.

Slowly the entire group of sliding kids gathered around Bridget and Ann.

"Can you get up?" Ann asked.

"I'm not sure," Bridget admitted. Her face was very pale.

"Let's roll on your side. Then we can see if you can stand from there."

As Ann gently helped Bridget roll on to her side, she saw the arm that barely looked like an arm, more like a coat sleeve with a tree branch trying to poke out. Bridget saw it too and began to weep.

"My arm," she sobbed, "My arm."

Patty pushed her way through the still growing crowd and stood staring at her hurt friend.

"Stay with her, Patty," Ann said. "I'm going to get help."

Patty nodded and Ann ran off. She needed to find one of the teachers on playground duty. They would know what to do.

Ann ran as fast as she could. There was a teacher near the school, watching the kids playing foursquare. Her stomach tried to climb up her throat when she realized it was Mrs. Kan-you-be-more-frightened.

Ann swallowed hard and kept on running until she was only a couple of feet away from her teacher.

"Bridget Malloy fell off the slide. I think her arm is broken," Ann belted out in one explosive breath.

"Go into the office and tell Mrs. Meyers what you told me. She'll know what to do."

Ann took off, "Don't run," a big booming voice called after her. "We don't need two injured students."

Ann walked swiftly to the office and delivered her message first to the secretary and then to Mrs. Meyers. The Assistant Principal flipped open the notebook on her desk, then picked up the phone and began to dial.

Ann walked swiftly back outside. She saw Patty walking Bridget through the playground, a swarm of students following behind them. Bridget walked gingerly, as if her feet hurt. She was holding her injured arm out in front of her with her other arm supporting it at the elbow. She looked as if she wanted someone to take her broken arm away and relieve her of all the pain. Bridget was still very pale.

"Everything is under control," Mrs. Kan-you-believe-what-happened called out. "Go back to what you were doing."

Slowly and reluctantly the students wandered back to

whatever game had only moments ago held their attention.

Mrs. Kan-I-help put one arm loosely around Bridget's shoulder and the girl nearly dissolved into the teacher's side. Together, teacher and student went into the building. Patty and Ann followed behind them.

In the office, Patty and Ann sat on a bench across from Bridget and Mrs. Kan-you-help-this-child. Bridget was leaning against the woman as if she were lounging in an overstuffed arm chair.

"Your mother is on her way," the teacher said smoothly, softly. "She'll take you to the hospital and they'll fix your arm. Everything will be fine."

Ann could not believe her ears. She had never heard her teacher use such a comforting tone before. Where was the big scary woman with the deep booming voice? Who was this imposter?

Within minutes, Mrs. Malloy appeared in the office doorway.

"Oh my word," she said as she took her first glimpse of her daughter's arm. "Thank you for waiting with her," she said and took the time to look the teacher and both girls in the eyes before she gathered up her daughter and left.

"If you girls don't feel like going back to the playground, you can wait back in the room for the rest of the recess." Patty and Ann nodded and stood up to leave. Their teacher had again used that soft soothing tone that Ann had never heard before.

Ann glanced over her shoulder at Mrs. Kan-you-believe-this-day. Ann hardly recognized her. She didn't look as big or as threatening as she had just minutes before.

Alien, was the first thing that popped into Ann's mind. She expected the woman's eyes to turn yellow or to see long green tentacles peek out from under the woman's skirt, but she was just sitting quietly on the bench, her ankles crossed and her hands gently resting in her lap.

CHAPTER TWENTY-ONE

Thanks

After Ann got home and she told Bridget's falling story to her mother and Marie, she went to her room and put away her books. Then Ann remembered the small square envelope Gail had given to her that morning.

Ann opened it. Inside was a small square card with a collection of Sponge Bob characters, each one sitting on top of the letters that spelled out T-H-A-N-K-S.

She flipped open the card and read:

Dear Ann,

Thank you so much for the frog. He is the perfect addition to my collection. It was a very thoughtful gift. I put him next to the swan.

Thanks again- your friend,

Gail

Your friend, Ann thought about those words. After all that had happened, that was what she most wanted.

It poured all morning; however Mrs. Kan-you-stay-dry's class didn't notice. They were busy making 'feel better' cards for their injured classmate. There was cutting, gluing, painting, folding and best of all, chatting. Ann later described it to Marie as a card-making party.

Mrs. Kan-you-get-this-done even brought in homemade cookies to devour while they worked.

"How are we coming on our cards?" the teacher bellowed; she was back to her usual menacing self.

"I'm done, almost done, done, almost," came a variety of voices from around the classroom.

"Cakes are done, children are finished," the teacher instructed.

"I'm finished, almost finished, finished, almost;"

"Much better," the teacher said as she watched her students gather up their trash and put away their supplies. "Bring your cards to me when you are finished."

One by one, the kids added their art to the pile on their teacher's desk. Mrs. Kan-you-believe-all-this-talent gathered up the cards and put them in a large manila envelope. She wrote 'Bridget Malloy' across the front and sealed it.

"Ann Taylor," the teacher roared.

Ann jumped up with a start.

"I have a job for you after school today." The whole class stared at Ann as the teacher spoke.

"Yes, ma'am," Ann squeaked.

"You live near Bridget, don't you?"

"Yes, ma'am."

"Good," the teacher boomed in a voice even louder than usual.

"Would you please stop by Bridget's house and deliver this?" The teacher waved the manila envelope over her head.

"Yes, ma'am." Ann sat back down relieved that this was a chore that she could handle.

There was no recess that day. The students were allowed to play outside in the cold, but not in the rain. It poured at a steady pace until an hour before it was time to go home and then the sun came out.

After getting her coat, Ann stopped by Mrs. Kan-you-do-me-a-favor's desk and picked up Bridget's cards.

"Thank you for delivering these for us," the teacher said in that foreign soothing tone.

"Sure," Ann said a bit confused and then she left, carrying the manila envelope.

Marie was waiting outside the school. They hadn't walked home together in a while and Ann was excited to have her sister at her side.

"We need to turn here," Ann explained as she pointed out the way to Bridget's house. "I have to stop at Bridget Malloy's house to drop off these get well cards."

"Great," Marie said and she followed her sister's lead.

"Bridget is sleeping," Mrs. Malloy explained when she answered the door.

"When will she be back at school?" Marie asked.

"Tomorrow, although she won't be allowed to climb the slide or swing on the swings for a while," Mrs. Malloy explained. "Bridget will have to take it easy for a while. Her arm is in a full cast and she can't risk falling again."

Ann handed the woman the envelope stuffed with handmade cards and the words 'Bridget Malloy' printed across the front. "I'll be sure to give her this when she gets up."

The Taylor girls said their farewells and started down the driveway. Something moving caught Ann's eye. She turned and stared at the front window. What had moved? Was it her imagination?

It moved again, like something waving at her. Ann kept looking.

"What are you looking at?" Marie asked and she stared too, not sure what she was staring at.

Ann could see into the front bedroom window, the same window that was her room at the Taylor house. She took two steps closer. She could see someone lying across the bed.

"There," Ann pointed toward the window.

It was Bridget lying on her back, her casted arm propped up by pillows. All the covers had been tossed aside and it was obvious that Bridget was sound asleep. On top of her chest lay what looked like a pile of dark wet rags. Ann could not see Homer's eyes, but every few seconds his tail would wag.

"That's Homer, their dog," Ann explained to her sister. "Look, he's made her so warm that she threw off all her covers."

Marie smiled. "Reminds me last year when you had the flu and King wouldn't leave your side."

The Taylor girls cut through the Malloy's yard and

then through their own. King was waiting at the back door. How did he always know when they were home? After each girl bent down and gave the pug's head a scratch, King ran off to find a place to nap. "Maybe I should take a board game or cards to school for Bridget to play," Ann thought out loud. "Doesn't sound like she's going to be able to play outside for a while."

After throwing their coats and backpacks on their beds, the girls went to the kitchen and took seats next to each other at the table. Mrs. Taylor put out a plate of cookies and two small glasses of milk.

"You should make up a game." Marie suggested.

"Make one up?"

"Like you did when we played Christmas."

"That was your idea," Ann stated.

"Not really," Marie explained. "You said Christmas would cheer you up. I just said 'let's do it'. You came up with all the details; the music, decorations, caroling, even the presents...all your ideas."

Ann thought about it. Marie was right; she had come up with all the details for their Christmas game. Ann thought about Bridget and what would be fun to do with a cast on your arm, but nothing came to mind. She would have to think on it more, later.

CHAPTER TWENTY-TWO

Oz

The next day Bridget was back. She had a cast that ran from halfway between her elbow and her shoulder all the way to the center of her hand. Lucky for her, it was her left arm and she was right-handed.

Before Mrs. Kan-you-believe-she's-back started the lessons, Bridget stood in front of the class. She looked tired and a little paler than usual.

"I wanted to thank everyone for the cards. They really cheered me up," Bridget said quickly and then returned to her seat.

At lunch, everyone gathered around Bridget to hear the details of arm setting and casting. Much of it she had to qualify with "At least that's what my mother said. I don't remember all that well".

Ann didn't try to penetrate the crowd. She sat off to the side by herself. Halfway through her sandwich, Kathy, Bridget's next door neighbor, plopped down beside Ann and started eating her lunch.

"Ann, right?" Kathy asked.

Ann nodded as Kathy peeled open her bologna sandwich and put several potato chips across the meat. She put the sandwich back together and took a huge crunching bite.

"She didn't want to come to school today," Kathy explained after she swallowed.

"Bridget?"

Kathy nodded.

"She looks worn out," Ann admitted.

"That'd not why. She feels stupid." Kathy took another big crunching bite.

"Stupid?" Ann felt confused. "It was an accident."

"Bridge feels too old to fall off a slide. Out of a tree, maybe, but off a slide is baby stuff."

"Those kids sure like listening to her story," Ann observed.

"For now," Kathy said. "Soon they'll lose interest, and she'll be all alone with that monster cast. Look how awkward she looks, like she's trying to salute or something."

Ann watched Bridget and her crowd for another minute. She looked tired and the mass around her kept swelling.

Through the rest of lunch Kathy and Ann talked about animals. Kathy planned to be a vet when she grew up. They talked about cats, lizards, birds, hamsters, dogs- anything that kids kept for pets.

"Bridget says you have some sort of monster dog. What's wrong with him?" Kathy asked.

"King's not a monster. He's a pug."

"Bug eyes, pushed in face?"

Ann nodded.

"Makes a lot of noise when he breathes?"

Ann nodded.

"Funny that Bridget described your King as a monster dog when she's got Homely Homer."

"I think Homer's cute," Ann admitted.

"So ugly he's cute." And the two girls laughed.

"Can I come over and meet King some time?" Kathy asked.

"Any time." Ann tried to hide her surprise as Kathy popped up, threw on her coat and ran outside.

One by one the crowd around Bridget thinned. Each

kid in turn threw on their coat and ran outside to play.

Ann waited to see what Bridget was going to do. Slowly she got out of her seat, walked over to the trash cans and tossed in her half-eaten lunch and then headed back toward the classroom. Ann followed her.

Mrs. Kan-you-believe-all-this-work was sitting at her desk grading papers. She didn't look up when Bridget walked in, as if she was expected, but she did glance up when Ann walked in.

Bridget walked to the window to watch the kids playing their games outside. She had a perfect view of hopscotch and the jump ropes.

Quietly Ann hung up her coat. She stood for a second watching Bridget, watching the playground. She looked so sad.

Ann walked to the window and pretended to be interested in the playground. Was Bridget staying in because she wanted to or because she was supposed to?

"It would be really bad if I fell again," Bridget explained. Bridget firmly rapped on her cast with her right fist. "Got to let the thing heal first."

"I brought cards and *Sorry*," Ann said, "in case you couldn't go outside."

Bridget said nothing, she just stared at all the

merriment going on outside.

"Do you want to play?"

"*Sorry*, maybe," Bridget said sadly. She wiggled the fingers hanging out of her cast. "Don't think I can hold cards."

Ann could have kicked herself; she hadn't thought of that. "I'll set up the board on the art table."

Ann went to her desk to get the game. She had stuck it underneath earlier and had hoped that no one would trip over the edges of the box that stuck out into the aisle.

"Ann, honey, can I talk to you?" Mrs. Kan-you-come-over-here said.

At first Ann didn't hear her; she was using that soft soothing tone that she'd used after Bridget's fall.

"Yes, Ma'am," Ann said as she made her way over to her teacher's desk.

"It was nice of you to bring indoor games, but look at her," the teacher said, motioning to Bridget who was still staring out the window.

Ann looked.

"Does she look like a kid who wants to play inside?"

Ann shook her head.

"Maybe, with a little encouragement and imagination, you could come up with something she could play outside, something where she won't fall."

Ann stared at her teacher's smiling face. This was not a scary woman; she was actually quite nice.

"How do you pronounce your name?" popped out of Ann's mouth before she could stop it. Her fingers flew to her lips as if she could catch the words and stuff them back in before the woman sitting before her heard them.

"Kan-u-czyn-squi," the woman said slowly.

"Could you write that down for me or I'll never remember it," Ann admitted.

"Ahh, yes, it's a tough one. My husband's family came here from Russia and some of their letters don't translate to English very well."

The teacher grabbed a pen and a small scrap of paper and began to print.

"K-A-N-U-C-Z-Y-N-S-Q-U-I," she wrote as she spelled. "Pronounced can-use-since-skey."

Ann stared at the paper. *Couldn't they fit an X in there,* she thought, but she said, "If you could only use names, that one would surely earn you a lot of points in Scrabble."

Mrs. Kanuczynsqui laughed a warm, friendly laugh.

"That's why I have the kids call me Mrs. K."

"Mrs. K?" Ann said in surprise. How simple was that?

"What about her?" Mrs. K motioned to Bridget who was still standing by the window. Ann turned and walked toward her.

"Let's go outside and play," Ann said.

Bridget just stared back at her.

"What do you say? We'll find something fun."

"It's so cold," Bridget's eyes filled with tears. "I can only zip my coat up part way," She wiggled her cast out in front as if Ann hadn't already figured out what got in the way. "This won't fit in the sleeve and I get too cold. You go ahead."

Ann thought for a moment.

"You wait here," Ann said as she gently squeezed Bridget's shoulder. "May I go to the office for a second?" Ann called to her teacher.

Mrs. K nodded and Ann took off.

All the way down the hall, Ann thought about Mrs. K and how stupid she'd felt. Why hadn't she asked any of her classmates about their teacher's name? And how silly she'd felt to have ever been afraid of this woman.

Once in the office, Ann went to the front desk and in a confident voice asked, "May I look in the Lost and Found?" Mark Minor appeared as if from nowhere. "This way, young lady, what exactly are you looking for?"

With her arms full of goodies, Ann swiftly walked back to the classroom. She dumped a pile of knit items out onto the art table.

"Grab your coat," Ann ordered excitedly. "I have a plan."

Bridget got her coat on and zipped it up as far as she could. Ann took two knit scarves, wrapped them around Bridget's neck several times and then tucked the remaining ends between the coat and Bridget's armpits. Then she took the rest of her Lost and Found treasures, twisted and tied, tucked and stretched until she had made a very crude yarn animal.

Ann used a stuffed black hat for a head, different color knotted scarves for the body and four mismatched mittens stuffed with the ends of the scarves to make four feet. Ann placed the yarn sculpture on Bridget's casted arm and tied one loose scarf piece around her elbow to secure it. It plugged the gap left by her open coat.

"What's this?" Bridget asked looking at what could easily be described as a big mess.

"Ever seen *The Wizard of Oz?*" Ann asked.

"Sure, who hasn't?"

"You are Dorothy, and that," Ann pointed to the bundle of scarves and such, "is Toto. Slide your cast over him some so he doesn't fall or blow away. As long as you hold on to Toto, you'll be warm."

Ann went and got her coat on.

"Who are you going to be?" Bridget asked.

Ann grabbed a couple of pieces of paper off the art table, wadded them up loosely and stuffed them into her hood. She pulled the hood up and zipped the coat all the way up. The paper made the hood stand straight up.

"Wicked Witch of the West," Mrs. K blurted out. Ann beamed. She had forgotten the woman was even there. Now all bundled up, Bridget and Ann walked out on to the playground.

After "I'll get you my little pretty," and "Auntie Em, Auntie Em," Patty and Gail came over to see what was going on and if they could join in.

MC

"You are the Scarecrow," Ann pointed to Patty, "and you," she pointed to Gail, "are the Tin Man. Your job is to hold on to Dorothy as you follow the yellow brick road, don't let her fall. Got it?"

The scarecrow and the Tin Man nodded.

"Are you warm enough, Dorothy?" Ann asked.

"Yup," Dorothy beamed as she, Toto, the Scarecrow and Tin Man skipped off towards the Emerald City.

After a few minutes, half of the playground was in OZ. Ann picked kids she'd never even met to be the Cowardly Lion, The Wizard, Uncle Henry and Auntie Em. Students of all ages were Munchkins, residents of Emerald City, castle guards, flying monkeys and talking trees.

When the bell rang several kids shouted, "Let's do this again tomorrow."

CHAPTER TWENTY-THREE

New

For several weeks the playground was transformed into Kansas, Munchkin Land, and The Emerald City. Then there was a noticeable change in the weather and Bridget began to complain about being hot.

Bridget wore a lightweight coat to school and left off the scarves from her neck. Ann made Toto smaller; but by the end of the week, the playground was back to swinging, sliding, jumping and running.

Patty brought her Chinese jump rope to school, and Ann and Bridget became rope holders.

"Even though I can't jump until this cast comes off," Bridget told Ann on the way home, "You can go ahead and jump. Someone else can stand with me."

"I can't," Ann said.

"I don't mind. I feel bad you're just standing there."

"I mean, I don't know how. I'd never seen or even heard of Chinese jump rope before we moved here."

Bridget thought about this as they walked. When they got to her front door she said, "Come over tomorrow and I'll teach you."

Ann looked at Bridget's cast and wondered how two girls, one in a cast and one who had no idea what she was doing were going to have a Chinese jump rope class.

"We'll get Kathy to come over and help us," Bridget said.

One morning the next week, after the usual announcements read by a student volunteer, Mrs. Meyers came on the intercom.

"Would Ann Taylor come to the office? Ann Taylor, come to the office." Mrs. K looked at Ann, no expression on her face and then pointed at the door.

Ann took a deep breath and headed toward the office. Mrs. Meyers was waiting for her at the office door.

"Come with me, child," the assistant principal said as she motioned for Ann to follow her. Ann trailed behind her. "Take a seat." Mrs. Meyers pointed to the chair in front of her desk.

Ann sat. Little beads of sweat began to collect around her hairline and she was having trouble swallowing. Why was she here? What had she done now?

"What do you call that game you had everyone playing at recess?" Mrs. Meyers asked.

"OZ." Ann meant to say more, but that was all that squeaked out.

"How do you play?"

"We act out scenes from *The Wizard of Oz*."

"Why that film?"

Ann began to get really nervous. Had she done something wrong? Was there some rule against acting out really old movies on school property? Why hadn't anyone told her? Just when she felt like she was fitting in, just when she had stopped watching and started doing...

"Everyone knows it. They know all the characters, the songs. Most people can recite many of the lines. That way more people can play." Ann found herself explaining.

"The more the merrier?"

Ann nodded still wondering what she had done wrong.

"We've gotten some phone calls," Mrs. Meyers said as she lightly tapped a pencil on the top of her desk.

"About OZ?" Ann swallowed as she spoke, trying to keep her stomach from tossing anything up and out.

Mrs. Meyers nodded.

"From kids' parents?" Ann was confused.

"Some parents and some grandparents."

Ann was stunned.

"They called to find out whose idea it was – this OZ game."

Why would they call to complain about the kids acting out *The Wizard of Oz* at recess? Ann's heart pounded. They weren't hurting anyone, just playing a game.

"I asked around and found out it was you."

Ann swallowed hard again. "Are they mad?"

"Mad?" Mrs. Meyers laughed. "They're thrilled."

Thrilled? Had Ann heard this woman correctly?

"They thought it was a creative use of the free time. It was all the kids talked about when they got home each day. Most of them wanted me to thank the student who organized the game; so on behalf of the parents and grandparents who called, thank you." Mrs. Meyers stuck out her hand and Ann shook it.

"They're welcome." Ann had no idea what else to say.

On the playground that day, someone had brought a Chinese jump rope and Ann was really excited to jump. She was next in line when she spotted a girl Ann had never seen before. She was standing way off to the side, watching the rope jumpers with great interest. She looked alone and sad.

"Who's that?" Ann asked.

"I don't know her name," Patty said. "But she's in my little brother's class. She just moved here last week."

Ann left the line and headed over toward the new girl. Another girl took her turn.

"Hi," Ann said and the new girl smiled. "My name is Ann."

"Susan." The girl looked terrified.

"You just moved here?"

Susan nodded still looking terrified.

"I've been here only a couple of months," Ann admitted.

Susan smiled and then looked down at her shoes.

"Who's your teacher?" Ann asked.

"Miss Ellis."

"Wow, Ellis, that's an easy name to remember. We call my teacher Mrs. K because her name is a spelling test all in itself."

Susan smiled again.

"Would you like to jump rope with us, Susan?" Ann asked. "It's really fun."

Susan shook her head.

Ann thought for a moment. "Do you like to jump rope?"

Susan nodded.

"Have you ever seen it done like that?"

Susan shook her head.

"Me neither, till we moved here. Would you like to learn?"

Susan shrugged.

"They call it Chinese jump rope." Ann leaned in closer to Susan. "I just learned how not long ago and if I can do it – you can do it."

Susan thought this over.

"Come on with me, I'll show you how and introduce you to the others."

Ann and the new girl walked together across the playground.

Made in the USA
Lexington, KY
16 March 2013